"Did I hurt you?"

Scott panicked as Dory emitted yet another strange whimper against his chest. "Dory?" He raised himself on one elbow.

Released from the weight of his body, Dory laughed fully, rocking with mirth. At last she said, "Hurt me? I feel utterly desired."

Scott brushed a strand of hair from her cheek and said, "I didn't plan—"

A fresh gale of laughter interrupted him. "No one could have planned that."

"You're sure I didn't . . . that I wasn't too rough?"

Her smile was as smug as the Mona Lisa's. "You just don't know what it does to a girl's ego to be able to incite a man to mindless lust."

"But what about you? You haven't. . . ."

"You'll make up for it sooner or later."

Scott slid his hand over her ribs to tease her left breast. "How about sooner?"

She combed her fingers through his hair and guided his face to hers. "How about now?"

Glenda Sanders claims that she's perfectly ordinary. . . "everyone's next door neighbor." Married to her college sweetheart, mother of two children, she would appear to be just your average middle American, except for one thing. Author of many magazine articles, columns and a dozen romance novels, Glenda has a unique gift. That gift is a talent for storytelling, demonstrated here in her second Harlequin Temptation, *Daddy, Darling*.

Books by Glenda Sanders

HARLEQUIN TEMPTATION
234–GYPSY

Daddy, Darling
GLENDA SANDERS

Harlequin Books

TORONTO • NEW YORK • LONDON
AMSTERDAM • PARIS • SYDNEY • HAMBURG
STOCKHOLM • ATHENS • TOKYO • MILAN

FORTY YEARS OF
Romance

Published July 1989

ISBN 0-373-25357-5

1

SCOTT HAD SHAMPOOED his hair and, with his eyes closed, was holding his head under the spray of the shower head. Feeling a sudden draft of cold air invade the steamy atmosphere behind the shower curtain, he stepped out of the flow of water and stumbled into the woman who'd just joined him in the small tub.

"Dory?" he asked, squeegeeing his face with his hand.

Reflexively throwing her arms around him to regain her balance, Dory said, "No. It's Norman Bates."

Her breasts crushed against Scott's wet chest. He slid his arms around her and spread his hands over her buttocks, pressing her body into his. "My, Norman, how you've changed." His lips covered hers, and his tongue probed inside her mouth immediately, possessively, hungrily.

The steam that surrounded them was only partly a product of the hot water spewing from the shower head. Dory felt Scott's manhood swelling against her stomach, and waves of answering desire pulsed through her womb. With one hand she reached past Scott to pick up the bar of soap from the soap dish. She slid it over his back with a circular motion, massaging the sleek, slippery wet muscles of his shoulders.

Scott kissed his way down her neck and circled her breasts with kisses before taking a taut nipple into his mouth, sucking at it, teasing it with his tongue. Groaning ecstatically, Dory danced her fingers over the sensitive nerve endings clustered at the small of his back.

Their bodies melded together languorously. Scott was fully aroused, and his erection pressed against her, hard, questing and persistent. The hand that had been at her breast moved lower and insinuated itself between them. He knew how to touch Dory, where to touch her.

As his fingers worked their sexual magic, Dory writhed against them. She sheathed his swollen organ with her hands. "Love me," she whispered urgently, squeezing his flesh with her fingers.

He said her name, repeated it. On Scott's lips, it was a caress, an endearment, an aphrodisiac. Gingerly he lowered her to the bottom of the tub and settled his body over hers. Hot water beat down on them from the shower nozzle, but they ignored it; they ignored everything but each other and the need for fulfillment that drove them.

Their bodies, slippery and wet and familiar with each other, joined smoothly. Dory crooked her legs around Scott's, embracing him, drawing him nearer as she arched against him. Half-floating in the soapy water that slithered sensuously over and around them, they moved in a frantic, exquisite, frenzied rhythm, kissing, sighing, groaning, urging each other on with the sounds of passion. Scott's palms kneaded her breasts while his mouth branded the soft skin of her neck; Dory nipped the tender flesh over his shoulder blade with her teeth and then sucked gently on his neck before his mouth found her mouth again and covered it in a searing kiss.

They found release, oblivion and paradise in the same instant. Dory's arms clasped even tighter around Scott's waist as she cried out her fulfillment, and Scott stroked her back soothingly, reassuringly.

Eventually he pressed his forehead against her breastbone, drew a lazy circle around her right breast with his forefinger and sighed raggedly. "Damn, you're so good."

Dory chuckled softly. "I was only planning on washing your back."

"If you ever decide to seduce me, I'm a dead man," he said. He blew a frivolous stream of noisy bubbles into the water slapping at his lips, then asked, "Do you think this is what it's like making love in the surf?"

"I'd say it's more like afterglow in a monsoon," Dory said, cognizant now of the shower spray beating down on them and droplets of water richocheting from Scott's shoulders onto her face. "Why's there so much water in the tub anyway?"

"One of us must have hit the plug," Scott said.

"Yes," Dory replied wryly. "*One* of us must have." Before he could react to her teasing, she sprang to attention, twisting past him to peek on the other side of the shower curtain. "Good grief!"

"The floor?" Scott asked.

"Are you familiar with the term *tsunami*?" Dory answered. She pressed her palms against Scott's shoulders and shoved gently. "Out, lover boy. We've got to get that floor blotted before Old Lady Viscount discovers water dripping out of her light fixture."

"Water can't penetrate laminated flooring," Scott said authoritatively. "It'll stand there until it's wiped up or evaporates." Dropping a kiss on Dory's temple and touching a spot he knew to be particularly vulnerable, he said, "Why don't I turn off the shower? We can pretend we're teenagers skinny dipping in the ocean."

"Scott!" Dory said, squiggling out from under him and reaching for the faucet behind him. "Honestly! If that water seeps though Old Lady Viscount's ceiling while you're fooling around . . ."

"We, Dory. We're fooling around. It's no fun alone."

"If Old Lady Viscount comes up here complaining about water in her ceiling, you're going to be the one who explains how this happened."

"If she's as nosy as you say she is," Scott replied, "she's probably already got an earful."

"Gawd!" Dory said, stepping out of the tub. "You don't really think she can hear . . ."

"Does a gator like dogmeat?" Scott said. He wrapped himself in the bath blanket Dory had hung on the towel bar for him.

Dory grimaced. "Don't start with the gator jokes, Scott. This is serious. We've got to get this water mopped up before—"

With a dramatic flick of his wrist, Scott flung the terry blanket from around his body, wielding it like a matador's cape. He bowed from the waist. "For want of a coat, m'lady." With that, he flung the large towel onto the floor.

Dory giggled, and Scott affected an offended pout. "You wouldn't have laughed at Sir Walter Raleigh?"

"Sir Walter Raleigh kept his pants on when he spread *his* cloak over the puddle," Dory said, kneeling to blot the floor with her own towel. "Look at all this water. How did we ever...?"

"It's that insatiable libido of yours," Scott said.

Dory planted her fists on her waist. "Libido of mine?"

"Wait until I tell Old Lady Viscount how you assaulted me in the shower."

"*Assault?* I'll give you assault!" Grabbing her satin sleep shirt from the vanity, she pummeled him about the head and shoulders with it. "Insatiable libido!"

Impervious to the attack, Scott captured the garment on a downstroke and yanked it out of her grip. "This looks absorbent," he said and, extending his arm full length, opened his hand. The whisp of satin floated to the floor like a feather plucked from a burgundy-colored ostrich. Dory and Scott watched as a spot of moisture stained the fabric and grew until the entire shirt was saturated.

They faced each other in challenge. Dory was the first to speak. "That," she said triumphantly, "was the shirt you like best on me."

Wearing only the naughty-boy grin Dory found irresistible, Scott said, "You won't be needing it."

Dory's gaze settled on the part of Scott's anatomy that proved he was ready to back up the suggestion in his tone of voice. She let it pause there significantly before smiling up at him smugly. "I guess I won't."

THE SOUNDS of a large man lumbering around in a small bathroom roused Dory just enough for her sleep-muddled brain to identify the source of the noise. Thinking, *Scott's here*, she contentedly snuggled her face a bit deeper into the pillow, holding on to the euphoric state of half sleep while she waited for him to return to bed and kiss her awake.

He placed the first kiss on the tender area behind her ear and worked his way to her lips. When her eyes were fully open, he slid his arm under her neck and put his head next to hers on the pillow. With their faces scarcely an inch apart, he smiled at her and said, "Hey, sleepy-head."

"Good morning."

"You planning on sleeping all day, or are we still going to brunch?"

Sliding her arm around his neck, Dory said huskily, "Neither."

What began as a gentle kiss intensified into a passionate one. Dory drew it to a surprise ending by rolling on top of Scott and straddling his midsection, pinning him, with the grace of his own acquiescence, against the mattress. Her palms traced the length of his arms from his shoulders down to his wrists, and she intertwined her fingers with his. "I think I'll keep you prisoner here."

From Scott's vantage point as he lay flat on his back, Dory's face high above him was framed by the silhouette of her bare breasts. He crooked his neck high enough to place a kiss in the alluring valley between the twin mounds of flesh. "Only if you promise to ravage and plunder me," he said and took a roseate nipple into his mouth. His tongue flicked over it, swirled round it; he drew on the flesh, aroused by the instant tautness of her flesh in response to his touch.

"I can't ravage and plunder you if you're ravaging and plundering me," Dory said. She slid her body lower along the length of his, wresting her breasts away from his mouth, then compensated the slight by pressing her lips over his and delving into his mouth with her tongue. She pulled her hands away from his to cradle his face with her fingertips, and felt his hands settle on her buttocks, kneading, pulling her into his hardness.

Gently, reluctantly, she lifted her mouth from Scott's. "I've got to take care of Dolly."

Scott groaned with the conviction of a man sorely tried. And frustrated.

"We don't want any surprises," Dory said.

Resigned to the delay in their lovemaking, Scott let his arms slide away from her body and sink into the mattress. "There are times when I wish you took the pill."

"Me, too," she said, dropping a kiss on the tip of his nose. "And this is one of them. But, I'm not, so . . ."

"Just hurry back, huh?"

In the bathroom, Dory removed her diaphragm. As she held the disk under the running water and lathered it with liquid soap, she tried to remember which of them had nicknamed the device Dolly, and couldn't.

Strange, she thought, the euphemisms that evolve between lovers. Dolly Diaphram seemed as much a part of her relationship with Scott as the unconventional routine they'd established. As she'd explained to Scott, it didn't seem to make sense for a woman to take a full cycle of pills every month when she only made love every other weekend.

Dory gave Dolly a fresh coating of spermicidal cream and put the diaphragm back in place. Then she washed her hands, brushed her teeth, splashed water over her face and applied a quick swipe of lip gloss. Her hair was wildly skewed from sleep, but she left it alone. Scott liked it mussed; he found it sexy that he was the only man who ever saw it uncombed and unruly.

He was waiting for her in the bed, with his elbow bent and his head propped on his hand. Impulsively, because she liked to surprise him, she dashed across the room wailing like a banshee and leaped onto the bed on top of him. She dropped a smattering of loud kisses on his face. "Time for the ravaging and plundering!"

Laughing, Scott said, "For Christ's sake, Dory, have some consideration for Old Lady Viscount's sensibilities."

"To hell with Old Lady Viscount's sensibilities," Dory purred, wriggling her body over his with feline grace. The sensibilities of the downstairs neighbor ceased to be a concern as she kissed Scott again, this time in earnest.

It was past one o'clock by the time Dory and Scott made it to brunch at the Tallahassee Hilton, and after three by the time they returned to Dory's apartment. Scott left soon thereafter so that he would reach the outskirts of Gainesville by nightfall. As always, although they didn't mention the time they would spend apart, their parting was bittersweet, the purity of their good-bye kisses tainted by the knowledge of the separation ahead of them.

Dory settled onto the couch with the Sunday paper, but it was a while before she could get interested in reading it. The apartment always seemed vacuous after Scott left, the rooms empty, the atmosphere dismal.

It took time for the routine of her life to ooze back around the void his absence created. Tonight the bed would feel too big for one person; she would hug the pillow Scott had used close to her body and still be able to smell his cologne. But tomorrow the dawning work week would leave her little time for such melancholy indulgences, and her busy law practice would be a demanding taskmaster.

Dory had no time for missing Scott. It was far more pleasant to use those rare moments stolen from concentration on her work thinking ahead to the next time they'd be together. Anticipation would carry her through the twelve days of romantic drought. It had to. That's the way things were when lovers lived so far apart.

2

As SCOTT PASSED the city limits sign, he looped his forefinger around the knot of his tie to loosen it. He sucked in a deep breath of air, released it slowly through his mouth and felt the tension of a hectic week easing from his neck and shoulder muscles. Friday afternoons were always good; they were even better when they preceded spending Friday night in Dory Karol's bed.

The rush traffic had thinned into the usual highway stream. Scott pressed his foot a little heavier on the gas pedal of his Mercury Cougar and switched on the cruise control. An expression of contentment that was not quite a smile softened his lips. A ninety-minute tape of carefully selected songs was reeling through the stereo tape deck, filling the car with his favorite music.

He gave a few fleeting thoughts to the term projects he'd assigned, and to one student who was trying hard but was still in danger of failing senior accounting, then let his mind wander to the woman who was waiting for him a hundred and fifty miles down the road.

Dory, short for Isadora. Her parents had named her after Isadora Duncan, but she'd had absolutely no aptitude for ballet. Nor had she inherited her mother's musical talent the way her sister had. Her propensity was the same as her father's: the law. John Milford Karol was a district judge, and Dory herself was in the process of building a prestigious law practice.

They had met three years earlier on a one-day cruise out of Port Canaveral. Scott had signed up for the excursion because he didn't have anything better to do, but he hadn't invited a date. Tired of playing singles games and burned out on the dating ritual in general, he'd gone alone, without realizing he was hoping something unexpected and magical and—yes—even romantic enough to impress a hardened veteran of the dating game would happen.

He hadn't known he was searching for romance when he wandered to an isolated deck to escape reggae music and the hungry, hopeful looks of young women shopping for male meat on the hoof. He'd thought he was seeking fresh air and peace, which he found.

He also found Dory.

She was standing with her hands on the railing, her head tossed back so that the brisk breeze swept over her face and swirled her hair back into a wild froth of curls. The wind was blowing her clothes, compressing the soft knit of her shirt against her breasts and lifting the sides of her matching culottes.

Scott stood for a long while just looking at her. He found her sexually attractive, but the attraction was more than purely physical. He tried to remember how long it had been since he'd been so intrigued by a woman, but couldn't. In addition to the decidedly carnal urges he got each time the wind lifted her culottes to grant him a glimpse of her upper thigh, he felt an intense desire to hear the sound of her voice, to see how her face would change when she smiled.

He moved to the railing, tilted his own face into the wind, sucked in a deep draft of sea air and said, "Now this is why you take a cruise."

"Ummm," she agreed, her voice rich and sweet as wild honey. She turned her face toward his, their eyes met and she smiled. Then, standing side by side, they turned their gazes back to the sea and let the sun warm their faces.

A brief exchange, a long, comfortable silence and unspoken agreement about what was important in life—such a simple beginning. But they were both already aware that what had begun would last beyond the ship's docking an hour before midnight.

The next time Dory spoke to him, it was to ask if his cheeks were normally so pink and offer him sunscreen from a bottle in her purse.

"You must do a lot of boating," he said, slathering the cream over his face. "You came prepared."

"Actually this is my first voyage. I just have sun-sensitive skin, so I keep a good sunscreen in my purse all the time." Spying a clump of cream on the side of his nose, she reached up to spread it into an even layer.

Her touch was gentle but efficient, and Scott looked forward to having her touch him in other ways, and speculated on how patient he would have to be before she did.

"This is my first cruise, too," he said. "I only came because of the special discount. I teach at the University of Florida."

"Uh-oh," Dory said.

Scott raised an eyebrow, questioning.

"I hail from a long line of Seminoles," she explained. "My father still takes his original stadium blanket to football games for good luck."

"I suppose that makes you an FSU alum?"

"Undergraduate and law school." She smiled at him again. The impact of it hit him like a fist in the guts. "But I'm the rebel of the family," she assured him. "I try to keep an open mind."

"Does that mean you'd let a Gator take you to lunch?"

LUNCH STRETCHED into a leisurely walk around the decks. Dory explained that she had been given a pair of tickets for the cruise by a grateful client. "I scheduled it for today so my sister could come. She's a senior in high school, and it was supposed to be sort of a pregraduation present. But an audition came up, so . . ."

"Audition?"

"Adelina sings," Dory said. "She's going to major in music next year."

"At Florida State," Scott guessed.

Dory nodded. "Of course. It would break Father's heart if she went anywhere else." She paused to watch the flight of a gull soaring overhead. When it had diminished into a tiny dot on the horizon, she looked back at Scott. "Adelina would never break Father's heart; she's the only one who came out right."

"What do you mean?"

"Well, my parents named my brother Sergei. For Sergei Rachmaninoff, the composer. Only Sergei turned out to have a tin ear, so he had to settle for becoming a surgeon instead."

"And you?"

"Dory. Short for Isadora, as in Isadora Duncan, the legendary ballerina. Unfortunately, I couldn't tell my right foot from my left foot when I started ballet class."

"So you settled for becoming a lawyer?"

"Just like dear ole dad—except that he's a judge now, and I'm still trying to make enough profit in my practice to pay down on my first BMW."

"And your sister—was she named after anyone special?"

"Oh, yes. Adelina Patti. She really wowed them in the opera halls in the mid-nineteenth century. It's an old-fashioned name, but it fits Adelina perfectly. She got the looks of an angel along with all the talent."

They walked and talked for hours, each sensing that they had been destined to meet, to become friends and, ultimately, lovers. They laughed together, rested over a sumptuous dinner, then danced on the deck in the moonlight. And later, just before the ship docked, they strolled back to the deck where they'd first encountered, and Scott Rowland became the first UF Gator Dory Karol had ever kissed.

They became lovers on their third date, and since then, the only distance between them had been measurable in highway miles—the one hundred and fifty miles that lay between Gainesville and Tallahassee. The physical distance kept their lives just separate enough to make their time together precious.

ONE WEEKEND A MONTH Scott drove to Tallahassee to share Dory's life. One weekend a month Dory drove to Gainesville to share Scott's. It worked beautifully, and had for nearly three years. There was no crowding in their relationship. No unreasonable demands, no nagging, no histrionic clinging, no boredom, no apathy, no fights over the family budget. There were only sharing and the sheer joy of being together.

Quite simply there was no one else on earth Scott would rather be with than Dory. He loved talking to her, he loved holding her or being held by her, he loved making love to her.

As the Cougar ate up the highway miles, Scott speculated on the weekend ahead. Oddly enough he and Dory seldom made plans together. Dory played hostess in Tallahassee, Scott played host in Gainesville. Surprise flourished in their relationship and breathed into it a life seldom sustained in long-lasting romances. Tonight Dory might meet him at the door dressed to kill and ready to party in some posh little night spot she'd heard about. Or she might not answer the door at all. He might find her sprawled on a pile of throw pillows in the middle of the living room floor wearing a sexy night shirt and ready for some very private partying.

A heaviness settled in his loins as he remembered past weekends and satin sleep shirts with peek-a-boo lace appliqués. Dory often wore satin. It suited her. It intrigued and aroused Scott. The vinyl steering wheel grew damp under his hands as he recalled the tactile contrast of slick, smooth satin riding the backs of his hands and firm, supple female flesh under his palms.

Their physical relationship was superb, explosive at times, tender at others. Years of togetherness had enabled them to learn each other's bodies, reach each other's needs, try new techniques, find shared ecstasy in the most basic ways of loving. The time they spent apart enhanced the sweetness of their lovemaking.

Anticipation was an aphrodisiac that heightened their needs and the excitement of their loving.

As usual, the last fifty miles turned into an exquisite torture of waiting. Memories of their lovemaking flickered through Scott's mind in a string of erotic images that titillated his senses. He could feel the coolness of percale designer sheets against his back, taste wine on Dory's lips, smell her perfume. Sometimes she lit a candle that surrounded them in a fragile cloud of that fragrance and projected their shadows on the wall as they coupled.

Impatience rode on Scott's shoulder until, at last, the thickening of traffic on the interstate signaled his approach to the city. He switched off the cruise control and leaned forward slightly, squinting against the glare of the sun settling like a ball of fire on the road in front of him. It was a relief to exit the freeway and turn so that the sun ball was to his side as he navigated the last mile to Dory's apartment.

The aroma of cooking food reached him as he stepped into the covered alcove in front of Dory's door. An irrepressible smile curled his lips. *They were dining in.*

Dory answered the door wearing a cowl-neck sweater, cord slacks and well-worn house slippers. Her teak-colored hair, which she smoothed back for the office and courtroom, curled frenziedly and untethered around her face, an indication that she had showered before changing into her casual clothes.

They were dining in, staying in. That was okay with Scott. It was dinnertime, and she was good company; he was hungry and Dory was a good cook. The world was good to Scott Rowland, Junior.

They kissed tenderly, briefly, confident that there would be time later on for passion. "Did you have an easy trip?" she asked.

"Uneventful," he said, "but long. It always takes too long to get to you." He followed her to the kitchen and leaned against the counter to watch while she stirred the gravy that was simmering. "You're right on time," she said, and then, "Nothing fancy tonight. Meat loaf."

"Mashed potatoes and gravy?" he asked.

Caught in the act of having included his favorite entrée in the menu, she smiled at him.

Symphonic cellists like Dory's mother taught their daughters to appreciate music, but not how to make a good meat loaf. Dory had learned to cook at the elbow of her best friend's mother, who was Southern to the core. Her basic meat, potatoes and vegetables menus suited Scott's tastes perfectly. When they wanted elegance, they dined out; when they wanted good food and a comfortable, homey intimacy, they dined in. He cooked at his house; she cooked at hers. It was another of the many pieces that fit so perfectly into the larger picture of their relationship.

"So how's life in Gator country?" she asked as they sat down to eat. In addition to being partner in a CPA firm, Scott taught part-time at his alma mater, but except for her reference to UF as "Gator country," and his referral to FSU as "that other school in Florida," the college rivalry caused only a teasing friction between them. Usually they made some outrageously sexy bet on the outcome of the annual UF-FSU grudge football game that made both of them personal winners and rendered the question of the final score in the game entirely moot.

"Typical of this time of year," Scott answered. "Everyone's still thinking football, but a few have begun to realize we're halfway into the semester. I assigned the term projects last week. Now the A students are driving me crazy with questions about picayune details, while the average students haven't even read the assignment sheet thoroughly yet. Same old routine. How about you?"

"We're scheduled to probate the Borten estate this week. Finally."

"I know you'll be glad to get that one cleared." The Borten estate had been coming up in their conversation for months now.

"We drew a reasonable judge," she said. "With luck we can get everything cleared in a couple of hours."

"Good," he said. He noticed, suddenly, the circles under her eyes which her makeup didn't quite hide. "You look tired."

"I am," she admitted with a weary sigh, as though she was relieved to get her tiredness out in the open, on record.

"Been burning the midnight oil in the law library?"

She shrugged her shoulders dismissively. "A little."

"You work too hard."

"Fine advice from a workaholic like you," she said, but he sensed a lack of conviction in her teasing, an absence of fun.

She *was* tired, Scott thought. She worked too hard. She always did. It was a family trait, either genetic or acquired. She had to have drive just to maintain her niche in that clan of overachievers from which she hailed.

His family situation was exactly the opposite. Scott had left home determined to break out of a mold of mediocrity, to become successful in the ways that mattered: money, prestige and meaning. Especially meaning. He enjoyed financial security and the trinkets money could buy. But he valued respect most of all, especially self-respect. He'd seen what happened to a man who loses his self-respect. It wasn't going to happen to Scott Rowland, Junior, the way it had happened to Scott Rowland, Senior.

He looked across the table at Dory and felt love and well-being and the realization of his good fortune swelling in his chest. This woman made no emasculating demands on him. She simply loved him, the way he loved her. Her strength, her independence were as appealing to him as the softness of her skin against his and the sweet scent of her hair when he buried his face in it. He loved her for that fierce self-sufficiency that was as much a part of her nature as her tendency to pamper him with tiny gestures that said, "I care about you."

"What?" she asked, catching him staring at her.

"I just like looking at you," he replied. "I missed you. I'm glad to see you. I think you're the sexiest woman on this continent."

She grinned. "You're horny."

"I'm contemplating making passionate love to you right here among the mashed potatoes."

"That could get messy."

"It could get interesting," he countered suggestively.

"I rented a movie," she said.

"We could watch it afterward."

"With mashed potatoes in our hair?"

"After a shower."

"Eat!" she said and, appraising the expression in his eyes, added with a sly smile, "Your dinner."

"We could have fun in the shower," Scott argued amiably, even as he plunged his fork into his mashed potatoes. "You could wash my back."

Again, he felt the thick warmth gathering in his loins as he watched the uncontrollable blush rising in her cheeks. How many visits ago was it that he was showering and she'd caught him off guard and they'd made love in the bathtub with the shower beating down on them? What an erotic adventure that had been!

Damn the movie she'd rented! he thought. He wasn't in the mood for a movie. He was in the mood for Dory.

Actually, he admitted to himself later, it wasn't so bad watching the movie. Having Dory cuddled in the crook of his arm and resting her head on his chest made him feel cozy and comfortable. It was relaxing—so relaxing that Dory fell asleep, and he had to nudge her awake with kisses on the forehead as the tape rewound in the VCR.

"I'm going to take a shower," he said. "Want to wash my back?"

Stretching, Dory shook her head and said, "I've got to get ready for bed."

Her look, the kiss she dropped on his cheek told him she was saying more than that she was going to put on her nightie and brush her teeth. "Getting ready for bed," when she said it just that way and gave him that knowing look, told Scott she would also be putting in her diaphragm. She knew it; he knew it.

She was waiting for him in bed when he got out of the shower. Tucked between old-fashioned rose print sheets and wearing pink satin baby dolls with ribbon ties and a smocked yolk, she appeared very young and innocent. The effect set the tone as they made love. They came together slowly, starting with the most basic of caresses under the covers, followed by gentle kisses and slow, subtle explorations of each other's bodies. They knew each other and each other's bodies well—where and how to touch, where and how to kiss to ignite the passion that led them to the ultimate physical union and the sating of their desire.

Afterward they lay together, arms and legs entwined, still and immensely satisfied, while their breathing and their heart rates slowed to normal.

At length Dory slipped her satin pajama top back on and resettled next to Scott on her side, pressing her back against his ribs. He reached up to turn out the bedside light and then cuddled next to her, sliding one arm under her neck, circling the other around her waist. Their bodies spooned together comfortably.

He loved the feel of her feminine curves fitted against him, her flesh against his flesh. Her satin pajama top was smooth and warm against his chest. He took a deep breath, inhaling the scent of her hair so close to his face. He kissed the top of her head, smiled in replete satisfaction as she snuggled closer with a contented sigh.

It might have been masculine instinct, the remnant of a primitive urge to protect his woman, that made him wait for her breathing to slow into the lethargic, regular rhythm of sleep before he allowed himself to surrender wakefulness. Or perhaps he simply enjoyed the sense of well-being he felt when she was sleeping next to him. Whatever the reason, he usually waited for her to fall asleep first.

Tonight, however, he waited in vain. After what seemed to be a very long time, much longer than it usually took her to drift off, he sensed that, although she was very still, she remained wide awake as she lay next to him. It was surprising, when she had been so tired earlier. He wondered if she had even closed her eyes, and suspected that they were wide open. He became aware of an alien tension in her muscles that disturbed him. "Dory," he whispered.

She made a tiny sound of acknowledgment.

"Are you all right?" he asked. "There isn't anything wrong, is there?"

Seconds stretched into and beyond a full minute while he waited for an answer. When she finally spoke, it was in a voice so soft that it hardly qualified as a whisper, yet he heard her as easily as he would have heard a shout.

"I'm pregnant," she said.

3

DORY KAROL had never known fear before. Oh, she'd experienced the normal anxieties inherent in the growing-up process. She'd felt that scalp-tingling type of anxiety a woman feels when she's walking to her car parked in an unlit parking lot on a dark night. She'd had her share of butterflies in the stomach before presenting courtroom arguments. But the fear lurking inside Dory Karol now was new to her, a hostile invader that permeated her mind and colored her thoughts.

It wasn't fear of carrying a child. She was a healthy woman, basically fit, and childbearing was a perfectly natural function of a woman's body. What scared Dory was change—change over which she had no control.

Up to the moment that she'd sat opposite her doctor and been told she was pregnant, all the change in Dory's life had been growth. She had progressed from childhood to adolescence, from adolescence to adulthood, from high school to college, from law school to law practice. All those changes had been positive ones, predictable ones, changes in which she'd had some freedom of choice. She'd selected her courses in high school, her major in college, the type of practice she wanted.

And then there was Scott. She'd recognized almost immediately that he was the perfect man for her. Eagerly she'd let him into her life; blissfully she'd surrendered her heart to him. From the very beginning they'd agreed that what they had was special, that their relationship didn't have to follow the traditional path to marriage, children and suburbia. They'd worked out the patterns that allowed their love to flourish despite the distance between them and the limited time they could spend together.

They were in tacit agreement that their relationship was as close to perfect as a relationship could be. It worked, so there was no need to change it. But now, because of the life tucked in her womb, everything was going to change. Her life. His life. Quite possibly, their love.

No, she thought frantically, *not their love. Not the way they felt about each other. Nothing could change that.* But as sure as Dory was that their love was sound, she was equally as sure that their relationship was in trouble. Love was the basic foundation, the solid slab upon which a relationship was built, but structure and design were important, too. And from the first, theirs had been an unconventional, experimental design. They were individual towers that met at specific intervals, not a single structure. Now they were facing a fierce storm of change, and who could say whether the experimental design could stand up under the strain? The fact that it might not, that their relationship might deteriorate under the pressure of an unplanned pregnancy, terrified her.

She might lose Scott. The very prospect of it, the horrible, menacing prospect, chilled her to the bone. She literally quaked in fear when she let herself think of it. Even now, when she had her body aligned against his and his arms were wrapped around her, that fear crept along her spine.

Scott's voice, explosive with incredulity, tore through the charged silence. "Pregnant?"

Unable to speak, she nodded her head, knowing he would feel the movement against his arm. Abruptly his arms were withdrawn and her head landed on the pillow with an ungracious thunk.

Seconds later light from the bedside lamp flooded over her face, making her feel like a prisoner about to be interrogated under one of those harsh hanging lamps with a metal shade. Scott had hitched himself into a half-sitting position with his weight resting on his elbow.

His face hovered inches above hers. Righteous indignation marked each of his features. His thick, dark hair was mussed in incongruous contrast with his outraged-inquisitor expression. "For God's sake, Dory! Pregnant? How?"

If it hadn't been so serious a situation, she might have answered him with a smart crack, a joke. He was *so* indignant, *so* outraged, *so* typically male.

But the situation *was* serious, and scarcely more than a week earlier Dory had sat opposite her doctor with close to the same expression on her face and asked exactly the same question: how?

Her doctor, with clinical detachment and wry humor, had replied, "The same way it's been happening since Adam and Eve set the precedent in the Garden of Eden."

Dory didn't have the luxuries of clinical detachment and wry humor. She said, simply, "It just…happened."

"It's impossible," Scott said. "We're always careful with Dolly."

"No method is one hundred percent fail-safe, Scott, even when you're careful."

Scott collapsed onto his back and let out a ragged, belabored sigh. "I don't . . . I can't believe this."

Softly, "I couldn't, either, at first."

There was a silence, a long, awkward, strained silence that hunkered between the parallel lines of their bodies on the mattress.

"I don't suppose . . . there couldn't be a mistake, a mix-up?"

"No mix-up. No mistake."

Another silence, then Scott posed *the* question: "What are you . . . what are *we* . . . going to do about it?"

Dory swallowed, trying in vain to get rid of the lump that had formed in her throat. "The doctor and I talked," she said. And then her voice did crack, as the first tears spilled over her cheeks. "I can't . . . *do something* about it, Scott. I just . . . I mean, the doctor was so blasé when he told me about a clinic where . . . but it's a human being, Scott, or it will be. I couldn't . . . hurt it. I couldn't just *get rid* of it like an . . . inconvenience."

Again that charged silence settled between them, an invisible enemy. Finally Scott said, "I'm glad . . . when you said that, just now, I was relieved."

He waited too long to ask, "Do you think . . . do you want to get married?"

Disappointment hit Dory with the force of an anvil dropped on her chest. He'd hesitated, and the obligation was audible in his voice. It took several deep breaths to make her own voice sound calm. "No."

"Dory. . ." he said, but she forestalled him. If she let him argue, let him offer to do the "right thing," she might let herself be convinced that it really was the right thing to do.

"Scott, the only valid reason for two people to get married is because they want to get married, not because of some outdated code of ethics."

"But . . ."

"I can deal with this, Scott. I'd be a hypocrite if I aimed this pregnancy at your head like an old-fashioned shotgun. I'm not some virgin you seduced in the hayloft. I'm a mature, independent woman who entered into a sexual relationship wholeheartedly. You've made it clear from the beginning how you feel about marriage, and I've accepted it. In fact, I've shared the same feelings. It would be wrong...disastrous...for us to start pretending to want what we've never wanted before."

Another pause, a small sigh. "Maybe you're right."

Dory closed her eyes against the tears burning them. She'd heard the relief in his voice. God help her, she could *feel* the relief in his body, feel it even though they weren't touching. She sensed it with an intuition that didn't require touch.

She despised Scott for that relief and knew she wasn't being fair. He hadn't had time to think about a baby, to adapt his thinking to include this uninvited event. Scott wasn't a family man. He'd never pretended to be. After the debacles his parents had made of their various marriages, he was altar shy, and justifiably so. She could hardly expect him to assimilate the news of his impending fatherhood in something under five minutes.

Pregnancy must have a muddling effect on the brain, she thought. Sometime in the past week, perhaps when she began to think of the baby as a human being instead of an error, a fantasy had formed in her mind. In the fantasy, Scott learned about the baby and miraculously discovered he was delighted.

How could she have been so blind, so stupid, so naive? Of course Scott wasn't delighted. Of course he didn't suddenly want to settle down not only to marriage but to parenthood, all in one fell swoop. You don't turn a hard-core bachelor into a doting family man by announcing, "Surprise! I'm pregnant." If Scott was feeling anything right now beyond shock, it was probably cornered; he would be feeling pathetically snared, like a coyote with his leg in the jaws of a steel trap.

She wanted to say something to comfort him, assure him, but she didn't know what to say; she wanted to touch him, but suddenly she didn't know how.

"Dory?"

"Hmm?"

"You know that I care about you, don't you?"

"Scott, yes. Of course I know that."

He reached for her hand and threaded his fingers through hers. "I'm glad you know."

A silent eternity followed before they fell asleep.

IN HIS SLEEP Scott turned to Dory, embracing her with his arms and legs. In her sleep, Dory cuddled against Scott, resting her head on his chest.

Upon awakening, Dory carefully extricated herself from his grasp—no easy matter with a sleeping male clutching her possessively, clinging to her when she tried to move.

Moments later the emptiness of the bed roused Scott. In the twilight of half sleep, he recognized the softness of Dory's bed, smelled the faint remnant of her perfume that clung to the bedding. He reached for her and found only an empty, lingering warmth under the sheets where she should be.

A vague unease hovered over his semi-wakefulness, as though he'd awakened in the middle of a nightmare that had left him on the edge of alarm. Slowly, as he came more fully awake, memories of the night before flooded back to him. Reality was worse than a nightmare, less escapable. Scott groaned into his pillow. What a mess!

He had not been consciously aware of the water running in the shower, but he noted the exact moment the pipes rattled in protest to being turned off. Lying still as death, he listened to the muffled sounds of Dory drying herself, dressing, toweling her hair.

He pretended to be asleep when she tiptoed through the bedroom. He needed time, a few minutes at least, to mull over the bombshell she'd dropped last night. It wasn't until he smelled brewing coffee and heard cooking sounds coming from the kitchen that he dragged himself out of bed and lumbered to the bathroom.

As he prepared to shave, he peered with self-loathing at the image in the mirror. It was a pleasant enough image, a conventionally handsome face. His hair was still thick and dark despite the traitorous strands of gray he discovered now and then. No, he had no complaint with the face or the hair. It was the man inside he loathed—the coward, the man who was less honorable than Scott Rowland, Junior, was supposed to be.

He loved Dory. He'd swear it on a stack of Bibles in any courtroom in the world. But marriage? A baby? That wasn't the way it was supposed to be, at least not for a very long time. Not until they were ready, if they ever were. They'd agreed. No legal pieces of paper. No pressure, no chains, no nagging, no regrets.

No babies.

Yet it had happened. Scott frowned mightily. Dory pregnant. The very thought of it made his stomach queasy.

For a moment after he lathered his face, he stared at the ridiculous piece of plastic he'd taken from the drawer Dory kept stocked with toilet articles for him and wondered if it was possible to slit one's throat with a disposable Bic. Not that he would. He wasn't feeling like much of a man, but he wasn't suicidal, only ashamed of himself. A woman like Dory. What kind of man wouldn't want to marry a woman like Dory after getting her pregnant?

A man who didn't want to get married at all, to anyone, that's who. Dory knew how he felt about marriage; she understood. She didn't want to get married, either. Hadn't she said last night that it would be a mistake?

Maybe it would be all right, after all.

Sure he thought, with the first deliberate swipe of the razor, it would be all right. And the sun would rise in the west tomorrow morning. Right after the cow jumped over the moon.

4

BY THE TIME Scott shaved and dressed, he was able to float to the kitchen on the aroma of baking blueberry muffins. Dory made them when she could find fresh blueberries at the supermarket, a hit-and-miss proposition in Florida. Ordinarily he would have commented on the special treat when he entered the kitchen, but today he was quiet. And, while he knew she'd undoubtedly heard him approaching, Dory didn't look up from what she was doing to greet him.

Scott's chest tightened when he saw her spine stiffen against the natural urge to turn to him, smile, tiptoe to kiss him on the cheek and tell him good morning. They were still the same people, yet they were different; the change in their relationship had left them uncertain of each other and, worse, uncomfortable with each other for the first time since they'd met.

Scott opened the cabinet and took out his mug. It was a familiar weight in his large hand, reassuring as he poured himself coffee at the coffee maker. Reassuring, until he looked down at it and read the caption he'd almost ceased noticing in the long months he'd used it: Super Stud.

Dory's matching mug said Super Broad. They'd bought them at a flea market, simply because they were so utterly tacky. Only now his was just strangely apropos in light of what he'd just learned. Scott slammed it on the counter in disgust, and the hot coffee sloshed onto the countertop and over his hand. He cussed and, plunging his hand under the faucet, turned on the cold water.

Dory looked at him, wide-eyed. "Are you okay?"

"Just stupid."

"Your hand—"

"The cold water will take care of it."

She stared at him questioningly, and he answered the unasked question. "Read the mug." He braced his hands on the edge of the sink and laughed bitterly. "Super Stud. That says it all, doesn't it? Mr. Macho, with sperm capable of penetrating rubber and surviving spermicidal jelly."

Dory closed her eyes, wincing. "Please don't, Scott."

He answered with a sigh. He looked down at his hands, and his shoulders sagged.

"It won't change anything," she said.

That was Dory. Always the pragmatist, pointing out the realities of a given situation. Scott wished he could be anywhere else at this moment, anywhere he could escape from the reality she wouldn't let him ignore.

He heard the cabinet door open, the rattle of dishes. Dory stepped behind him and slid her arms around his waist, offering him the cup and saucer in her right hand. He took it, then covered her left hand with his, pressing it into his ribs. She kissed his nape, then snuggled her cheek against his shoulders. Her breasts pressed consolingly into his back. "We don't have to talk about it now," she said. "It's going to be months before I'm even showing. Until then—" She drew in a shuddering breath and lifted her cheek from his shoulders. "Why don't you have some coffee."

"How about you?" he said.

She lifted a glass from the counter and said, "Orange juice. I'm off caffeine."

"Oh," he said. Of course. Caffeine wouldn't be good for a baby. He drank heartily from his own cup, as though the hot coffee might burn away the despair closing in on him.

Dory peeped into the oven to check the progress of the muffins. Apparently satisfied, she took out a skillet. "Do you mind cooking your own eggs?" she asked.

Scott cast her a surprised look. Cooking eggs was no big deal, but he couldn't remember Dory ever having asked him to cook for himself at her apartment. She was a whiz with scrambled eggs, beating them just right, whipping in a smidgeon of milk so that they were fluffy, adding just the proper trace of pepper.

Dory handed him the carton of eggs. To his questioning look, she said, rather embarrassed, "I'm not...I haven't had a lot of trouble with nausea, but for some reason, raw eggs—"

Scott put the carton back into the refrigerator. "I don't need eggs."

"It's okay. Really. As long as I don't have to see them raw. There's no reason for you to give them up."

"Cholesterol," Scott said.

After a beat they both laughed. Dory had been lecturing Scott about cholesterol ever since they'd met, and he'd consistently turned a deaf ear. It had become a joke between them. Scott touched Dory's neck and traced the line of her jaw with his thumb. "It feels good to laugh. I wasn't sure we ever would again."

Dory closed her eyes and nodded agreement, then stepped into his embrace. She put her arms around his waist and her cheek against his chest, savoring the familiar warmth of his solid body, hearing the regular pumping of his heart beneath her ear, smelling the combination of her soap and his after-shave. Scott. So familiar. So dear. Involuntarily she pressed nearer to him, closed her arms to hug him tighter.

They didn't talk. They didn't need to. Everything they would have said was telegraphed in the way their bodies touched with an unself-conscious familiarity.

Scott pressed a kiss on her forehead, then picked up his cup and saucer and went to the table to drink his coffee. Dory watched the muffins until they were done then popped them into a napkin-lined basket and carried them to the table.

"What are we doing today?" Scott asked, after buttering and devouring one of the muffins and reaching for another.

"I didn't make any plans," Dory said. "What do you feel like?"

"The weather's nice," Scott said. "Something outside, maybe? The Junior Museum?"

"I'd like that," Dory said.

"We could take in a movie afterward," he said, and she nodded agreement.

It was an unhurried day. Dory rejoiced in the freedom of cotton pants, an oversized T-shirt and sneakers in lieu of the business suits and pumps she wore during the week. They followed the nature trail at a leisurely pace, stopping from time to time to soak up the peacefulness of the outdoors. When they talked, it was to point out something along the way—a bird perched on a limb, a squirrel flirting with them from the far side of a tree.

Content in the serene surroundings of the museum grounds, they skipped lunch altogether, opting for an early dinner on the way to the movie. On the way home, Dory tried unsuccessfully to stifle a yawn and hoped Scott wouldn't notice in the dark interior of the car. But he did. "Tired?" he asked.

"Um," she said, yielding to the inevitability of another yawn. "Must be all the fresh air today."

"Must be," Scott agreed. But they both knew fresh air didn't usually make Dory tired, and an awkward awareness of the real reason for Dory's fatigue reverberated in the air between them.

When they reached the apartment, Dory excused herself to change into a kaftan. Although she hadn't mentioned it to Scott, the elastic waistband of her slacks had turned into a vise. She returned to the living room and found Scott watching football on television. "You should have told me the Gators were playing," she said, dropping onto the couch next to him. "We could have skipped the movie so you could watch the first half."

Scott grinned and leaned over to kiss her briefly on the lips. "No football game is as important as spending time with you."

"Except maybe the Georgia game," Dory teased. "Or the Florida-Florida State game."

"That one, we go to together," he said, draping his arm around her shoulders.

"Father still can't get used to my sitting on the Gator side," she said. "You'd think I'd defected to Russia."

"You just saw the light," Scott said. "Now switching from the Gator side to the Seminole side—that would be worse than defecting to Russia."

"You're almost as bad as he is," Dory said. "You're both little boys when it comes to that stupid college rivalry."

"I'm on the Gator payroll, darling."

"I can almost understand your attitude, since you've never really left college. But Father's been an alumni since before I was born, and he still can't say 'Gator' without prefacing it with 'damned.'"

"I'd be willing to bet he can't say my name without prefacing it with 'that damned Gator,' either," Scott said.

"He uses the term with affection," Dory said. "He likes you, and you know it. Despite your connection to that little school in Gainesville." She cozied closer and let her head drop against the inviting warmth of his chest. Scott ran his hand up and down her arm and kissed the top of her head. "Careful. You might fall asleep."

"Um," Dory agreed, succumbing to the lethargy slowly seeping through her muscles. She was nearing deep sleep when Scott's chest vibrated under her ear. "Have you told them yet?"

"No." An awkward silence followed. "I wouldn't tell them before telling you," she said softly. "I wouldn't do that."

Scott made a strained clicking sound of frustration in the back of his throat. "Don't be surprised if your dad comes up with a few more colorful names for me after you do. 'Gator' will be an endearment."

"My family knows how it is with us," she said. "They aren't going to—"

"They're not going to be thrilled."

"They'll be shocked," Dory said. "Just like I was. The way you are now. But when they think about it—"

"When they think about it, they'll be hopping mad as hell, and it won't be at you."

She sat upright to face him, nose to nose. "They aren't going to be mad. They're going to be surprised. And then when they think about it, they'll realize—"

"Ha! You're their daughter, Dory. And I'm the man who knocked you up."

Dory drew in an involuntary shriek. "Is that what how you think of this . . . situation? That you 'knocked me up'? What we have is not a seedy one-night stand, or a tacky little affair—"

"I know that."

"Then I wish you wouldn't talk about a . . . a new life in such vulgar terms."

"I was just being realistic about how they're going to see this, Dory. Don't expect your mother to take up knitting."

A laugh rose up in Dory's throat, part bitterness, part incredulity. "My mother would be a menace to society with a pair of knitting needles."

"I wasn't trying to be funny."

"You weren't succeeding."

They glared at each other a moment. Finally Scott drove his fingers through his hair and groaned. "Why, Dory? What we had was perfect. Why the hell did this have to happen?"

After a very long silence, Dory stood up and looked down at him. "I'm tired, Scott. I'm going to tuck in early."

"Do you want me to go with you?"

"Go ahead and watch the rest of the game. I hope the Gators win."

Neither of them bothered with good-night.

Early the next morning Scott sat in the chair at Dory's makeup table staring at Dory. Asleep, she looked small and vulnerable in the double bed. Her face was childlike in repose, and her hair painted a dark slash on the light pillowcase. He tried to see something different about her, something that flashed the fact she was pregnant, but it was too soon for that. Sleep had even erased the dark circles under the eyes. She was simply Dory—the same Dory he'd fallen in love with on the cruise ship.

Why? he thought. *Oh, Lord, why did it have to happen?* And what was it going to do to their relationship? And how was he ever going to deal with it?

Dory woke up and caught Scott looking at her. He was fully dressed. "Good morning, sleepyhead," he said.

"What time is it?" she asked groggily.

"Ten-thirty."

"Why didn't you wake me up?"

"You needed the sleep."

Memories of their conversation the night before crowded into Dory's consciousness as she shook off the last remnants of sleep. She closed her eyes. The memories didn't go away, so she opened them again. "Brunch?" she asked.

"One of us is on the verge of starvation," Scott replied drolly.

"Give me twenty minutes."

"I'll be in the living room reading the comics," he said, rising.

He was almost through the door when Dory asked, "Did the Gators win?"

"Yes," he said. But there was no satisfaction in his voice.

Despite her hearty appetite and the lush spread of fruits, vegetables, meats, breads and cheeses, brunch that day was quite possibly the most miserable meal Dory had ever endured. Scott appeared to be just as miserable as she was, picking at his food and grimacing at his first taste of the coffee. Their attempts at conversation fell short, turning into clipped exchanges that made them both uncomfortable. Dory dropped a dollop of grape jelly on her skirt, and Scott somehow tipped over the cup of coffee he hadn't drunk, then dabbed ineffectually at the spill while the dark stain spread pervasively over the white linen cloth.

"Do you want dessert, or do we leave before we knock over a serving cart or two?" Scott asked.

"I vote for leaving," Dory said. "I don't recall seeing anything on the dessert table that blended with grape-jelly purple."

The quiet in the car was even worse. Until Dory sighed miserably and Scott reached over to fold his hand around hers. Until he drew both their hands back to rest cupped together on his thigh. Until he leaned over at a stop light to kiss the tear stains on her cheek.

He embraced her when they reached the parking lot at her apartment, and she put her arms around his neck and buried her face against his neck and hugged him as though he'd just rescued her from a burning building. His arm was across her shoulders as they walked to her door.

Inside, they clung to each other and kissed frantically. They had tasted the possibility of losing all that was special between them, and now had been granted the hope of recovering it. Scott lifted his lips from hers and whispered urgently, "I can't leave without loving you again."

Together, almost as though their separate bodies were appendages of a singular being, they walked to the bedroom and took off their outer clothing. Scott adored her nearly naked body with his eyes, then, while kissing her, unsnapped the front closure of her bra and cupped her breasts in his hands. Dory gasped, and twisted away just slightly. Scott lifted his head and gave her an inquiring look.

"They're a little sensitive," she said. "It's normal. Just . . . be gentle."

He guided her to the bed and they lay down together. He touched her breasts again, lightly this time, then took the tip of one in his mouth when it swelled under his palm. Dory arched against him, explored the length and width of hard muscles on his back. They shifted so that he was atop her, and her body moved under his in gentle undulations of invitation. Impatiently Scott shoved his fingers inside the elastic of her panties and shoved them down. Dory cooperated, kicking them away, then opened to him.

Urgently Scott shed his own underwear and then buried himself in her. She locked her legs around his, holding him close. They moved together frenziedly until he spilled himself inside her, then lay atop her, breathing heavily while his heart pounded noticeably against her sensitive breasts.

Dory combed her fingers caressingly through his hair and pressed soothing kisses on his forehead and temple. Eventually he slid away from her, yielding the ultimate intimacy but leaving his thigh over hers and his arm across her waist. "Did you—" he asked.

"No," she said. "But it's okay. I enjoyed it."

He raised his large hand to cradle her face tenderly. "Do you know how special you are?"

She put her hand over his, stroking the back of it sensuously. "It's special with you," she said. And though she couldn't tell him, that made even a baby seem right. She had known immediately she couldn't destroy his child, the child they'd created together. And now she knew that she would love it, no matter what.

He leaned forward to kiss her, and then, gently, began touching her with arousing brushes of his fingertips while his mouth plundered hers. His hand eased lower, stroking, until he eased his finger inside her. She gasped into his mouth as the heel of his hand settled over her and then moved, playing her body like a fine instrument, creating the friction he knew from experience would bring her the same magic that had just consumed him. Everywhere he touched her, every way he touched her was an affirmation of caring. Dory grasped his shoulders in a desperate grip, clinging to him as the world telescoped into pure sensation.

She cried out as the spiral waves of magic convulsed through her. Her body tautened, then eased against his; her hands caressed instead of clung. The strokes of his fingers soothed rather than aroused. Dory's breathing slowed to normal as she listened to the reassuring pulse of his heart close to her ear. Her last cognizant thought before she succumbed to sleep was that sweetness so profound could produce nothing except sweetness.

Dory awoke to the flirting sensation of tiny kisses on her eyelids. When she opened her eyes, Scott smiled down at her.

"I fell asleep," she said groggily.

"I hated to wake you up, but it's almost four."

"Four?" she said incredulously. "It can't be. Oh, Scott, I'm sorry. Our time—"

"It's all right. I've had you next to me." He shifted, and his swelling penis pressed against her thigh. Dory reached for it, wrapped her hand around him lovingly, stroking, felt him lurch and expand within the circle of her fingers. His sigh had an aphrodisiac effect on her senses, arousing her. Still caressing him, she buried her face in the hair on his chest, then sought the flat nipple on his right breast and teased it with her tongue. It hardened, and she sucked on it.

Desire surged through her as his flesh pulsed under her hand, and a growl of male arousal tore through his throat. He rolled back, urging her astride him, and guided her face to his, hungrily accepting the plunder of her tongue as they kissed. Dory eased her moist warmth over his waiting erection and gasped as he filled her. She set the rhythm as Scott squeezed her firm buttocks, guiding, urging, controlling.

She was the first to climax; her thighs, flanking his, pressed into solid muscle and hair-sprinkled male flesh as she convulsed with the force of orgasmic ecstasy. After several suspended seconds, Scott rolled her under him and pumped into her frantically, claiming, dominating as he found turbulence, then peace.

For a long time after he collapsed over her, neither of them moved. Then Scott, softening abandonment with soft kisses, slid off her and sat up, dropping his feet over the edge of the bed.

"You don't have to get up," he said softly.

"As if I could," she murmured lethargically and smiled up at him.

He walked to the bathroom, then brought her a wash cloth and stood patiently while she laved the moisture of their lovemaking from between her legs. Later, after he'd showered, dressed and packed, he brought her the Sunday paper and kissed her on the forehead. "I'll see you in two weeks."

Dory nodded, afraid to trust her voice because of the lump in her throat. By the time he'd reached the bedroom door, however, she'd swallowed the lump and risked calling his name. He stopped and turned back to look at her. Dory discovered that she didn't know what to say. They stared at each other for almost half a minute, then spoke at the same time.

"Dory—"

"Scott—"

Scott exhaled heavily and ran his left hand through his hair. He was holding his suitcase in his right hand.

"I'll be all right," Dory said. A lame platitude. It was the best she could do.

"Sure," Scott said and squared his shoulders. "Well—"

Dory conceded defeat. "See you week after next."

Scott hesitated. "Dory—"

"Just go. Please."

Still he hesitated, lingering in the doorway as though his decision to cross through it would be irrevocable. Finally he mumbled, "'Bye," and took the definitive step.

5

PREGNANT. Scott was trapped inside the car with the word during the long trip home. To him it was a word packed with unpleasant connotations. He couldn't associate it with Dory. He couldn't relate it to himself, to Scott Rowland, Junior. It couldn't have happened; it just couldn't have. They were too careful. Things were too good between them to have everything fall apart with an "accident."

Pregnant. No matter how high he turned the volume on the tape deck, the music wouldn't drown out the word. It wasn't a mistake, not a cruel practical joke. Dory was pregnant. And he was responsible. What was it going to do to them?

Involuntarily his mind reverted to the first time that word had torn his world apart. His mother was screaming it at his father, and his father was screaming back. Seven-and-one-half-year-old Scott Rowland, Junior lay awake in his bed trembling, wondering what the shouting meant. His friend Alvin's mother had been pregnant, and now Alvin had a baby brother. Was he, Scott, going to have a brother?

Scott didn't think so. Alvin's mother had been happy about a baby, not mad. And Scott was hearing another word being shouted in the next room, an ugly, ominous word that made him shiver despite the weight of the covers: *divorce.* Scott lay still, afraid to move for fear he'd miss something, a word, a phrase, that would enable him to make sense of what he was hearing.

It would be a long time, months and months, which to a child seemed more like forever and forever, before he would understand the full significance of that argument. But even though he didn't understand, he knew, with a child's unerring intuition that something terrible was happening, something that threatened the foundations of his life.

"Your daddy's gone," his mother said, when his father didn't come home from work the next night.

"Gone where?" Scott asked.

Bitterness sharpened his mother's voice as she said, "Gone for good."

Days later, Scott asked, "Is Daddy dead?"

His mother harrumphed. "No such luck. If he was dead, there'd be insurance, and I wouldn't be having to hunt for a job."

"Will I ever see him again?"

"If he wants to see you, I might have to let him."

Two weeks later, Scott's father was waiting for him after school on a Friday afternoon. Scott was so relieved to see that his father really was alive that he dashed into his father's arms, and clung to him, saying "I missed you, Daddy," over and over again.

"I've got good news," his father said. "You're going to spend the weekend with me."

It was true. Scott's mother had packed a suitcase for him, although she seemed to resent having to do so.

"This is where I live now," his father said, unlocking the door to an apartment with rooms so small it reminded Scott of a dollhouse he'd seen once. But the most surprising revelation during Scott's visit was a woman named Melinda, who had curly blond hair and smelled like the perfume counters at the front of department stores.

"Melinda lives here, too," Scott's father said.

Scott shook the hand Melinda offered, but her presence confused him. He had an instinctive grace that made him wait until he was alone with his father before he asked, "Do you like Melinda better than Mother?"

His father looked very sad. "I used to love your mother, Scott. But your mother and I, well, we're different people than we were a long time ago when we got married. We want different things. Melinda and I have worked together at the office and ... we do want the same things. I didn't mean for this to happen, Son. Sometimes we can't help the way we feel. Melinda and I are more alike than your mother and I are."

Scott was trying to be big. He didn't want to cry. But he felt the humiliating wetness on his cheeks and wiped them with the back of his hand. "Do you love her more than you love me?" he asked. "Is that why you want to live with her now, instead of with me?"

His father hugged him again. "I love you, Junior, and I'll never stop. Your mother and I can't live together anymore, but that doesn't mean you and I can't still be close." It felt good to hear his dad call him Junior, the way he always had.

"You can come visit me," his dad continued, "and we'll do things together. Would you like that?"

"Will Melinda be here all the time?"

"She lives here, Scott," his father said. "And she wants to get to know you." He paused, reading the emotions on his son's face. "But sometimes we can go do things together. Man things, like ball games or go-karts. How's that?"

Scott nodded because he knew his father would be disappointed if he didn't agree. But he wasn't at all sure Melinda wanted to get to know him, the way his father had said. He didn't think Melinda liked him, and he didn't like Melinda much.

Back at home, he told his mother about Melinda and instantly regretted doing so, because it made her angry. "So," she said, "you met the slut."

Scott could tell "slut" was an ugly word because of the way she said it.

"I suppose she's pretty," his mother said.

Afraid of angering his mother further, Scott just shrugged his shoulders.

His mother looked at him suddenly and cocked her head at an angle as she studied his face. "You look just like your father. You always have. I wonder if the bastard will, too."

Bastard. Another new word. It would be months before Scott linked the new words to Melinda's swelling abdomen. Melinda was pregnant; that made her a slut; her baby was a bastard; his parents were getting a divorce.

That was his mother's version. His father's version was quite different. He said Melinda was a beautiful, loving woman, and their baby was not a bastard, because Scott's father married Melinda the day his divorce from Scott's mother became final, which was several days before Scott's step-sister was born.

Torn between conflicting attitudes, Scott didn't know whom or what to believe, so he formed his own opinions.

Very quickly he developed the habit of keeping his opinions to himself. It became a matter of self-preservation for a child torn between battling parents and step-parents, a child struggling to keep his father's love from being usurped by step-siblings, a child watching his parents destroy themselves living with bad choices and irrevocable consequences.

Pregnant. Like the echo of the word shouted over two decades before, it was sounding in Scott's life again, threatening as ever, powerful as ever, destructive as ever.

DR. LATHAM was doing the usual probing and poking of Dory's abdomen as she lay on the examination table. "Any problems?"

"I don't think so," Dory said. "Nothing out of the ordinary. I still tire easily."

"How about morning sickness?"

"A little more lately than before, but not too bad."

"Well, I could prescribe something for nausea, but I advise my patients to avoid drugs and take the crackers route unless the sickness becomes unbearable." He motioned for her to sit up. "You tell the father about this baby yet?"

Dory sobered noticeably. "Yes."

The doctor's stare was fixed on her face, waiting for more information. When it was not forthcoming, he prompted, "Well?"

"It looks like I'm in this solo," Dory replied.

"I want to see you in my office when you're dressed," he said abruptly and stalked out of the room.

Nice bedside manner, Dory thought caustically, climbing off the examination table and shrugging off the ridiculous examination smock.

Dressed, she stepped across the hall into the doctor's inner sanctum. Was this routine? She thought the monthly exam was a cursory prodding and probing and a "See you next month." When the doctor walked in some fifteen minutes later, she asked, "Is everything okay? With the baby, I mean."

"You're a textbook case," Dr. Latham replied drolly. The leather cushion whooshed and the wood and springs groaned in protest as he settled into the chair behind his desk. "It's a perfectly normal pregnancy."

"Then why the private conference?"

"You're two weeks away from the end of your first trimester," he said.

She nodded. "That's the crucial time, isn't it? I mean, if I haven't had trouble yet, there's a good chance I won't have any trouble at all?"

"You've been reading."

"That sounds almost like an accusation," she replied. "I just like to know what's going on with my body. Is that a problem for you?"

"The question is," the doctor said, "is it a problem for you?"

"I don't understand what you're driving at, Dr. Latham."

"You're obviously interested in your pregnancy, Dory. I just want to be sure that you're aware of the end product. You tell me you're in this pregnancy—What was that clever little phrase you used? I believe it was 'solo'."

"I don't believe this!" Dory said. "You're disapproving of me because I'm not married. You're my doctor, not my minister! What right . . . ?"

"Whoa!" the doctor said, holding up his hand like a traffic cop. "Slow down. Hear me out before you start getting self-righteous. I couldn't care less whether you're single or married or living with seven dwarfs."

Dory gave him an impatient, disgruntled little sniff and folded her hands in her lap contritely. She'd been referred to him by a friend who'd been going to him for ages and ages. Maybe she needed someone a little younger, with a more contemporary perspective.

"I know what you're thinking," he said, as though reading her mind. "But I've been taking care of pregnant women for a long time, and I've seen thousands of them, in thousands of sets of circumstances. So if you'll grant me the wisdom that comes from such vast experience and hear me out—"

She nodded to him, as if acknowledging his point with a silent *touché*.

He continued, "You're a smart woman, Dory. And you're open to new experiences. Right now being pregnant is an adventure, and going 'solo' is a challenge. But when you get to the point you can't see your toes and realize you're going to have a baby to deal with, you're going to have second thoughts. You're going to panic, and wish you'd thought this through now, before it was too late."

"You're wrong," she said.

"Am I? You told the father, thinking deep down he was going to want to get married and play papa. Well, he didn't. And believe me, because I've seen this situation hundreds of times, that if he didn't turn papa as soon as he heard, he's not going to join the team further down the road."

"I don't care," Dory argued. "I can take care of a baby. A lot of women raise children alone, and I'll have it better than most. I can afford to make a home for this child, and I know I'll love it."

"Have you ever spent much time around children?"

"My younger sister."

"How much younger?"

"Five years."

"That's not enough space to give you perspective. You were a child when she was a baby. No nieces or nephews?"

Dory shook her head.

"You'd better give this some more thought," the doctor said. "Borrow a baby for a few days and get a taste for what you're in for. It's not playing house. Parenthood means round-the-clock accountability. You can't put a child on hold when you have a tough case in court or a special date."

"I'm not naive, Dr. Latham. I'm not some starry-eyed teenager who thinks I'm getting a real live baby doll. My biological clock is ticking—"

"You've got plenty of good years ahead of you, young lady. Panic is no reason to have a baby."

Dory felt the heat of anger in her cheeks. How dare he question her decisions, try to play God in her life! "How dare you question my decision or try to play God in my life!" she said.

"I'm trying to point out reality to you, young woman. Two weeks from now, one of your major options will be closed to you. Abortion at this point would be a simple, safe procedure."

Tears were burning Dory's eyes. Too filled with nervous energy to sit in the chair another second, she bounded out of it. "I do not want an abortion. Even Sco...the father...was relieved when I told him I wasn't considering an abortion."

"If he knows about this child, and has decided to let you 'go solo,' then this man has relinquished his right to tell you what to do about this pregnancy."

"He has more of a right than you do," Dory said.

"I wouldn't be so sure of that," Dr. Latham said. "He's feeling relief for his own conscience. I'm thinking about you, and what this child will do to your life. It's not going to change his life appreciably. You're the one who's going to have to make all the accommodations."

For once Dory had nothing to say, no refutation. Deflated, she dropped back into her chair.

The doctor got up, walked around the desk and leaned against the edge of it, looking down at her. His voice was soft, placating. "If you'd come into my office last month on pins and needles hoping you were pregnant and then rejoiced in the news, I'd have kept my counsel today. But you were shocked, and not what I'd call immediately overjoyed. You didn't decide to have a baby... you're just afraid to decide not to."

He pulled away from the desk and walked behind her chair and put his hand on her shoulder. "Two weeks, Dory. It's not my deadline; it's nature's. You think about it. You think about it long and hard. And don't go running to the *abstentia* father for advice. It's your body, and your decision. But I don't have to tell you that. I'm sure you've read the feminist propaganda."

Dory's hands were trembling as she unlocked her car. She didn't know whether which she was more of—humiliated or infuriated—but she was glad she'd scheduled her appointment late in the afternoon so she wouldn't have to go back to the office afterward. She longed for the solitude of her apartment, the peace waiting for her there.

When she arrived, she locked the door behind her, kicked off her shoes and exchanged her suit for a kaftan before collapsing into the billowing softness of her sofa. Peculiarly, though she hated the tearfulness that seemed to accompany pregnancy, she wished she could cry. Her head ached with the pressure of the tears she'd held in check in the doctor's office. But she couldn't cry.

The solitude of her apartment closed in around her, cloaking her reassuringly, and the tension in her muscles began a gradual easing. The fan motor of the refrigerator hummed in the kitchen, and a water pipe creaked as someone in a distant apartment turned on a tap: familiar sounds breaking through the absolute silence to render it friendly.

Dory seldom watched television, often forgot to turn on the stereo. She enjoyed the cocoon quiet of the space she called home. She tried to imagine this space, this normally tranquil place, filled with the noises of childhood. A baby's cries, the bumps, bangs and rattles of toys, the whirring of the washing machine agitating around clothes stained with strained whatever it was babies ate.

The proverbial pitter-patter of little feet, she thought, mocking her own ignorance and naïveté. Panic breathed hotly down her neck. Was she ready for a baby, an invasion of her quiet space, her ordered life? Because of her career, she seldom had time for company. The only person she'd shared her home with, with any regularity was Scott.

Scott. Suddenly she longed to talk to him, to hear his voice, feel the human warmth of his body next to hers. Her body, her life, perhaps even her soul, was on a schedule accustomed to Scott's presence every other weekend. Tomorrow was Friday. Tonight she would pack for her trip to Gainesville. She was aching for Scott, and not just in the physical sense. That last strained attempt at conversation in her bedroom was the last time she'd heard his voice. Sometimes they called each other between visits; sometimes, when they were busy with their respective careers, days passed and they realized they hadn't.

She was desperate to talk to him, to know what he was thinking, how he was dealing with the idea of her pregnancy, but she wanted to give him time to deal with it, time and space in which to establish a perspective. Scott was an introspective person, a brooder.

What would he have thought about the scene with the doctor, she wondered. Would he have been as incensed as she over the idea of scraping away their child? Would he have cared? *Oh, Scott, would you care, or would you be relieved, the way you were when I said I didn't want to get married just because of the baby? Do I want this child enough to raise it without you?*

She picked up the phone and dialed the back line at his CPA firm. His partner, Mike, answered, and seemed surprised to hear her. "He's at the campus this afternoon. It's Thursday, remember?"

"Of course," Dory replied. "I've been kind of busy. I guess I lost track of the week."

"You might catch him right after class at his office on campus. Or I could try, and tell him to give you a call."

"That's okay," Dory said. "I'll call him at home tonight."

"Nothing urgent, I take it."

"No. Nothing urgent." *Only our lives, our love. Our child.*

"How's Tallahassee? Is the cloud of hot air still hanging over the state capitol?"

Dory managed a small laugh. "It's still there. The politicians keep it replenished."

"You're coming in this weekend, aren't you?"

"I think so." *Think?* Hadn't she just been thinking about packing. Since when wasn't she sure?

"Why don't you talk Scott into bringing you by the house while you're here? Susan's always asking why we don't see more of you."

"I'd enjoy seeing her. And the baby. How old is she now?"

"Nine and a half months."

"She must be getting big."

"She's learning to walk."

"That must be . . . very special."

"Dory, you're all right, aren't you? You sound a little distracted."

"I think I might be coming down with something," Dory said. The possibilities of what she was coming down with seemed endless: cowardice, selfishness, self-doubt.

"I hope not. I'm sure Scott's looking forward to seeing you this weekend."

Dory bit her lip to keep from asking if Scott had said so, if he'd mentioned this weekend in particular. She wanted to ask if Scott seemed distracted lately, if he seemed thoughtful, if he, too, was asking about Mike's baby, wondering what it was like to have a nine-month-old daughter who was learning to walk.

She wanted to say, *Oh, and by the way, did Scott mention I'm pregnant?* But it wouldn't be fair to Scott to pump his business partner and best friend for information, so she said, "Maybe we'll see you," and followed it closely with a good-bye.

She hung up the phone more frustrated than ever. Frustrated, tired, confused, and . . . hungry. She'd been too nauseated to eat this morning, and too busy to eat lunch. Now her body was signaling that, despite emotional turmoil, she needed fuel to keep herself and another life going.

Nothing in the fridge or pantry appealed to her, so she traded her kaftan for baggy jeans and a long-tailed shirt, pulled on her oldest sneakers and went out in search of food. She wasn't sure where she was headed— hell, she wasn't sure about anything, why should dinner be any different?

She was starting to hate making decisions, especially the nitpicking little ones like whether to head for a market for food to take home and prepare, or to go to a restaurant and let someone wait on her. Maybe she could go over to the Adam Street Commons. Was she dressed well enough for Andrews Upstairs? Just the thought of Andrews made her hungry for mesquite-grilled chicken. The Melting Pot might be easier to get in and out of. She could start with a cheese fondue and veggies, then maybe progress to shrimp or chicken, and finish up with fruit and angel food chunks dipped in chocolate.

Half a block ahead she spied the golden arches of a McDonald's. There was a playground out front, with several children climbing on brightly painted gym equipment.

Borrow a baby, the doctor had said. Not having a baby to borrow, she'd do the next best thing. Besides, she hadn't had a Big Mac in years. She hit the brake and executed a hair-pin turn into the McDonald's lot, ignoring the irate driver behind her who honked angrily and flashed an obscene gesture with his hand.

The uninitiated would have captioned the scene inside Feeding Time at the Children's Zoo. Unconsciously Dory had been seeking children, and she'd hit the mother lode. Parents and children were everywhere. The woman in front of her held a squirming toddler and attempted to corral two older children while ordering a family dinner that included three Happy Meals.

The toddler regarded Dory with curious, blueberry-pie eyes over his mother's shoulder. Dory stared back at the child just as curiously, noting his slightly pug nose, his pink bowed lips, the errant curl of his thick brown hair. His wide-eyed expression was expectant, waiting.

Reflexively Dory smiled. The toddler smiled back cunningly. In that instant, Dory wanted to hug him so badly that the deprivation of not being able to do so left a metallic taste in her mouth. *Maternal instinct*, she thought, and wondered at the strength of the phenomenon.

An argument broke out between the older children over who would carry the tray to the table, and the mother turned to referee, moving the boy from Dory's line of vision. The family stepped aside en masse, still haggling, and the teenager behind the counter asked for Dory's order. Dory's response was automatic from her college days. "I'll have a Big Mac, fries and a diet—no, make that a shake."

"What flavor?"

"Chocolate," Dory said, feeling deliciously indulgent. She had been giving the overhead menu a cursory read-over. "You have salads now," she said.

"Yes ma'am."

The deferential response from the teenager was jarring. Was she suddenly so ancient that teenagers called her "ma'am"? "I'll have a salad, too," she said, and then had to review the menu to decide what type.

A man had joined the family haggling over getting the trays to the table. He said, "What seems to be the problem here?" The two children answered him at once, but he seemed to grasp the essence of the disagreement with the efficiency of an electronic radar unscrambler.

"You guys," he said, shaking his head, marvelously indulgent. He gave each of them a boxed Happy Meal and pointed them toward the seating area. "Here. Now go find a table." He shot his wife a grin and put out his arms in invitation to the toddler. "Come on, Joey."

Joey—the little beguiler—went to his father, and his mother picked up the tray and followed her husband to the table. Dory, still waiting on her food, followed with her eyes. The man was quite ordinary, pleasant looking, slightly thick in the waist. His shoulder muscles strained the back of his shirt as he carried the boy in his arms. A daddy, stepping in as the marshmallow authoritarian.

Oh, Scott. I've never thought about it before, but you'd be so good at being a daddy. Dory herself had had a "father," not a daddy. She had been loved and respected, but never coddled. The thought of her father the judge at McDonald's was as ludicrous as the idea of her mother taking up knitting baby booties.

Scott's father would have been the daddy type, had he not been torn apart by conflicting loyalties. Otherwise he could not have hurt Scott so; only a person who inspires love has the power to hurt a person that way, to jaundice his attitudes the way Scott's were.

Dory had met Scott Rowland, Senior, once, and her lasting impression was of sadness haunting his eyes. He'd looked older than his true age, and walked with his shoulders stooped. Marriage to a maniacally possessive, compulsively jealous, domineering woman exacted a heavy toll from a man.

"Here you go," the teenager said, sliding the tray of food toward Dory. Dory carried it to a two-seater table near the windows overlooking the playground. She bit into her two all-beef patties, tasted the horseradish tang of the special sauce and savored the divinity of a triple-decker sesame seed bun. The fries were hot and crisp; the shake, thick and luscious. How could she have forgotten how wonderful fast food could be, she wondered, as she tore open the envelope of salad dressing and squeezed it over her salad.

Having eased the edge of her appetite, she turned her gaze to the playground, paying close attention to details of the slice-of-life scene outside—the clothes the children wore, the scowls of concentration on their faces as they played, the way they interacted with their peers, their siblings and, on the fringes of the play-ground, their parents.

The distinct personalities of the children fascinated her. Simply by watching them play she identified leaders and followers, adventurers and brooders, introverts and extroverts. She imagined them in courtrooms: the brooder sitting in the swing soberly pondering the world would be a judge. The little boy dangling precariously from a window in the spaceship could grow into a flamboyant showman who would charm a jury with wit. The little girl urging a younger child up the steps of the slide would be the type to seduce a jury with soft-spoken persuasion. The adventurer at the top of the space ship would be an aggressive prosecutor.

It was unconscionable to lump these little beings into a collective group and tack a single label on them. These weren't *kids*, they were young individuals, each with a unique personality, perspective and wide open potential. Were they born so different, or were they molded into introverts and extroverts, daredevils and dainties by their parents?

The full realization of the sacred trust parents inherited with the birth of a child swept over her. What an awesome responsibility, to let a child be the person he was born to be while helping him to be the best version of that person. The very thought of such responsibility was sobering.

Unconsciously Dory pressed her hand over her abdomen. The tiny life in her womb weighed scarcely an ounce, but it was safe for now, floating in a warm sea of fluid, an inimitable protective, climatized ocean ingeniously designed by nature. Could she keep it safe later, after it left that rarefied atmosphere and became dependent on her in a whole new way? *Could she do it alone?*

She had finished her food. She tossed the cartons and napkins in the trash can, and walked outside to the playground. The tables here were low and shaped like flowers. She sat down and took a long draft of her shake. The little girl who'd been coaxing the smaller child up the steps of the slide came running over to the next table.

"Jenny went down the slide," she announced to a woman who was reading a paperback book.

The woman put down her book. "Yes. I saw that."

"She didn't want to go, but I showed her how."

"I saw you helping her."

"I'm going to show her the spaceship."

"That should be fun."

The child's body was tensed with hope. "Can we stay for hours and hours?"

Her mother laughed. "Another ten minutes."

"Mom!" the child protested. "That's not long enough."

Her mother's eyebrows flew up. "You'd better go enjoy the time you've got."

"But—"

"Re-bec-ca."

The girl's face pinched into a grimace of displeasure, but she turned and ran toward the spaceship, where the younger child was waiting for her. Within seconds the two of them were starting up the ramp that led inside.

"That was a short-lived rebellion," Dory commented to the mother.

The woman chuckled. "Amazing, isn't it?"

"Are they both yours?"

Shaking her head, the woman said, "The little one is my niece. She's staying with us while her parents are on a trip."

"Your daughter seems to be taking her in hand."

"Rebecca thinks Jenny's one of her baby dolls, only better. She's been mothering her to death."

Dory tried to remember if she'd ever had a baby doll, but couldn't recall any. She'd gone through a Barbie phase during her preteen years. Her Barbie had had a town house complete with a pool, and a horse. *Why couldn't she remember a baby doll?*

"Which one is yours?" the woman asked.

Dory shrugged sheepishly. "None of them. I just . . . I've been thinking about having a baby."

The woman gave her an interested look. "It's a big step, isn't it?"

"Yes. A very big step. And . . . irrevocable."

The woman laughed. "No returns allowed."

"Was having children a difficult decision for you?"

"No," the woman said somberly. "We'd been trying for years. I had two miscarriages, and we were beginning to lose hope that I would have a full-term pregnancy."

"How awful for you."

"It was awful at the time." She brightened visibly, "But now we have Rebecca and the doctor says there's no reason I can't have another, so we're hoping again."

"How old is Rebecca?"

"Four."

Rebecca and her cousin had reached the first level of the spaceship and waved through the round hole. Her mom waved back.

"She's very pretty," Dory said.

A smile claimed the woman's entire face as her gaze lingered on her daughter. "Yes, she is." She turned back to Dory. "Of course, we try not to make a big deal of it. We don't want her to be conceited."

"There's a lot to motherhood," Dory thought aloud. So many things to consider, to weigh one against the other. So many decisions to make.

"Yes," the woman agreed. "There's a lot to it. It's not a simple job."

Dory had more than enough to think about. She stood up. "I've got to go. I hope..." She wasn't sure how to wish someone luck with a pregnancy.

"If it's meant to be, it will be," the woman said, understanding the sentiments Dory hadn't been able to express.

The words, spoken so calmly and with such assurance, stayed with Dory as she drove to the mall, where she bought several books on pregnancy, and continued on with her to her apartment.

If it's meant to be, it will be.

6

SCOTT DID NOT even hang up the receiver between phone calls, just depressed the button long enough to break the connection with Mike at the office, then frantically dialed Dory's home number. Snatches of his conversation with Mike drifted through his mind as he listened to her phone ring. *"Probably nothing... sounded a bit distracted... coming down with something... thought you'd want to know she called."*

Guts constricting, he gave up after a dozen rings. *Where are you, Dory? At the hospital?* For a long time he sat at his desk, tapping the tips of his steepled index fingers against pursed lips as he fretted, oblivious to the hurrying and scurrying of the students beyond the closed office door. *Dory, please be out shopping, picking up your cleaning, buying panty hose—anywhere but at the hospital.*

After the last class of the day, the campus hunkered down to sleep like a tired giant, steeling itself for the boisterousness of the next class day. The noise of students dwindled to an occasional footfall or hushed exchange in the hallway. Scott paid the silence no more notice than he had the earlier confusion.

Probably nothing... not feeling well..." Yet Mike had been concerned enough to call Scott and tell him about the call.

Probably nothing . . . Yet something in Dory's manner, her tone of voice, had triggered Mike's concern. Scott knew Dory too well, knew how private she was, knew she wouldn't have told Mike if something was terribly, terribly wrong. But she'd called his CPA office on Thursday afternoon, even though she knew he would be at the college. Dory didn't make mistakes like that. Scott dropped a hand to the phone, closed his fingers around the receiver, then realizing the futility of it, released it. It was too soon to try again. He'd wait awhile, then redial.

The idleness of waiting left him vulnerable to an onslaught of memories he'd long kept stored in the back of his mind, unpleasant memories that disturbed him even now because of the emotions they brought back to him so vividly.

He was nine, older and ever so much wiser than he had been at seven when he overheard an aunt talking to his mother. "A baby? Beth, have you lost your everloving mind?"

Her voice, raised in disbelief, drew his attention. Scott lost track of *Gilligan's Island* at this bizarre turn in their conversation. He dared not turn away from the television for fear of betraying his eager interest in what they were saying at the dining room table, but he listened with the intensity of a desperate child.

If what his aunt was saying was true, it meant his mother was pregnant. He knew that word now, it and all its insidious implications and complications and ramifications! His mother pregnant? It was unthinkable. Unforgivable. An unfathomable betrayal that made her recent marriage pale in significance. Holding his breath, Scott waited for his mother to refute what his aunt had just said, to correct the mistake, to take away the knot of nausea the news had tied in his young guts.

His mother said, "I haven't lost my mind, Cynthia. I'm playing it smart this time."

"But you know how much trouble you had carrying Scott Junior. You know what the doctor said."

"Yes. So I didn't have any other babies. And look what happened. Scott Senior left me."

"Scott was fooling around with his secretary and got caught, Beth. He was chasing a skirt, plain and simple. It had nothing to do with your not having more children."

Scott's mother harrumphed. "That bitch has been dropping babies like a brood mare, and Scott loves it. Well, I've got a second chance at marriage with Mel, and I'm not repeating the mistake I made with Scott. Mel wants children."

"If he wants children at the risk of your health, then he's not much of a man."

"You don't know him."

"I'm not sure you do, either, Beth. You met him what—three months ago? I think you're wearing blinders where he's concerned. You were desperate for a man, and he came along."

"You don't know what it's like being alone, Cynthia. You've never had a husband run off on you."

"Look, if you love this man, and he loves you, then that should be enough."

"But Scott—"

"That's it, isn't it? You're still trying to compete with Scott's new wife. Can't you see how futile that is? She's ten years younger than you are, Beth, and she doesn't have the female problems you have. You're not going to prove anything but your own stupidity if you try to have a baby."

"*If you try...*" Scott breathed a little easier. That must mean she wasn't pregnant. Yet.

"This discussion might be academic at this point," his mother said.

A fresh onslaught of goose bumps crawled up Scott's spine. He didn't know what academic meant, but it didn't sound good.

"Lord, Beth. Please don't tell me that," his aunt said, confirming his worst fears.

"I'm late."

Late for what? Scott thought.

"Well, God help you," Aunt Cynthia said.

It was the beginning of a new phase of the nightmare.

Frantic, Scott tried to push away the memory of his mother's long and troubled pregnancy and dialed Dory's number again. When there was no answer, he decided to go somewhere for dinner. Food might ease the gnawing pain in his gut, and it wouldn't hurt to have a solid meal under his belt, just in case he had to make an unscheduled trip to Tallahassee.

THE PHONE roused Dory from deep sleep. She reached over the arm of the sofa for the phone on the end table, sending the books in her lap tumbling to the floor. "Ho?" she said groggily.

"Dory?"

The urgency in his voice was alarming. "Scott?" she asked back.

"Dory, are you all right?"

"Oh. Oh, sure. I was... I was reading and I must have dozed off."

"I've been trying to get you for hours. Mike said you'd phoned the office."

Good old Mike. "I forgot it was Thursday."

"He said you thought you might be coming down with something."

"I'm just a little tired. The doctor says it's normal, but I didn't want to go into it with Mike."

"Oh." A pause. "Well, I'm glad it's not the flu or anything."

Say something about the baby, Dory thought. *Tell me you're glad it wasn't a problem with the baby. Tell me you weren't hoping...*

"You're still coming this weekend, aren't you?"

So they could both talk around the fact that she was carrying a child? So she could vent her rage at her doctor's attitude and watch Scott not react? "I... Scott, I could really use some extra rest. The slugfest over the Borten estate really took its toll."

Dory found the total silence with which she was answered unsettling. She said awkwardly, "It's still a critical time, Scott. And the drive—"

More silence. "Please say something," she pleaded.

"I miss you, Dory." Another prolonged silence stretched through the line before he asked, "Do you want me to come there?"

If only you could come and we would talk about the baby. Our baby. The baby I'm getting to know, the one my body's already accommodating. If we could talk, if we could plan together, if I could tell you what the doctor said and be sure you'd be as outraged as I was....

"I . . . maybe that wouldn't be such a good idea," she said.

Fear swelled inside Scott, a different fear from the one that had made him frantic to get in touch with her, but no less urgent and, certainly, no less intimidating. He was losing Dory; and they were losing to awkwardness that special closeness they'd always enjoyed with each other. Pregnant. And now she wasn't coming to see him, didn't want him going to see her. God, but it hurt. It was a physical pain tearing at him, this regret, this wishing nothing had changed, this wondering why it had to happen.

"It's probably better this way," she said softly. "I really do need some rest, with the holiday coming up. And I think you need a little more time and space."

"I need you, Dory."

Dory closed her eyes. *Tell me that you want our baby. Tell me that you need it, too, because it's a part of us.* "Oh, Scott," she said, fighting back the uncharacteristic tears that were always so close to the surface now. "I need you, too. But . . ."

"Listen to us, Dory. This isn't the way it's supposed to be with us."

"That's why. . ." She said it too quickly, then sighed wearily. "The truth is, I want to talk about the baby, and I don't think you're ready to, and I don't have the stamina to spend the whole weekend pretending it doesn't matter."

"God, Dory. Do you know how good it feels when you level with me like that? Like some giant wave of relief."

"You're not angry then? About this weekend?"

"Disappointed. Not angry."

And not ready to talk, Dory thought. In his own way, Scott had leveled with her, and she, too, felt relief mingling with disappointment.

"Are you still going to your mother's for Thanksgiving?" she asked.

"I have to. Duty."

"I was hoping..." She took a breath. "I've been thinking while the family is all together, that it might be a good time to tell them. I thought maybe you might want to be there."

"I don't know what to say, Dory. It's your family."

And my baby? she thought bitterly. *Mine, not ours?*

"You'll have to decide how and when to tell them," Scott went on. "If you want to wait until the next time I'm in Tallahassee, then we can tell them together."

"I'll give it some thought."

"Dory—"

"Scott—"

They laughed self-consciously, mirthlessly.

"We're doing it again," Dory said. "Acting like strangers."

"Silly, isn't it?"

"Yes. Oh, Scott, I wish we could be together and just hold each other and not have to talk at all."

"Couldn't we?"

"I don't think so."

"You're probably right."

"We'll be together weekend after next."

"Another two weeks will seem like an eternity."

"Two weeks always seems like an eternity. That's why we don't talk about it. Rule number one of a long-distance relationship, remember?"

"Damn the rules, Dory!"

His irritability earned a chuckle from her. "Mike said you were getting lonely. You really do get grouchy when you've been away from me awhile, don't you?"

"Irritability is a perfectly normal male response to sexual deprivation."

"For that, you get a little something extra next time we're alone together," Dory purred.

"That two weeks is getting longer all the time."

"For what it's worth, even though we're not supposed to talk about it, you're not the only one who's lonely in that respect."

"Then why, Dory?"

"The only answer to, 'Why,' is, 'Because.' It would just be impossible right now. We'd both be hearing what we weren't saying."

"I don't have to agree with you, do I?"

No. Please. Argue with me, her mind pleaded. *Tell me you're ready to talk about the baby*. But he'd already admitted he wasn't.

"It's going to be a long weekend," he predicted sadly.

Dory regretted her decision to cancel her trip to Gainesville almost before the receiver was back in place. The weekend hadn't even started, and it was already too long; it yawned ahead of her like a sentence in solitary confinement. How could she deliberately have denied herself Scott's company when she needed him so desperately? Surely avoiding the subject with Scott wouldn't be as awful as tackling it without him.

She coped by focusing on herself and the baby, sleeping, relaxing, reading, carrying on a one-sided conversation with the life within her. She missed Scott, longed for him in all the small, significant ways a woman yearns for the man she loves, for his touch, his understanding, his wit, for the special sharing of two people who love and respect each other.

In the period of self-imposed exile from him—a weekend she ordinarily would have spent with Scott, a weekend she spent instead alone with the child forming in her womb—she faced the harsh reality of the changing timbre of her life. Scott always had played an episodic role in her life. He came to her like intermittent rays of sunshine stabbing through swaying tree branches, bursting with passion and romance. Their relationship to date had hinged on freedom; freedom to function within their separate lives, independent of each other; freedom to merge separate lives at set intervals knowing they could let go when it was time to let go.

A baby would curtail the freedoms upon which their relationship had been based. While the quality of their love was not in jeopardy, the structure of their relationship was. No matter how they clung to the feelings they had for each other, their relationship might not be able to withstand the strain of distance without the freedom to move in and out of each others lives without having to answer to anyone else. Her heart constricted at the thought that, no matter how much they cared, they might drift apart. It would be a gradual parting, a slow goodbye, like a lingering death by degenerative disease.

Again she found she was pressing her hand over her womb, unconsciously protecting the tiny life within her. *Oh Scott, can't you see it's eventually going to be all or nothing? Why are you making me choose?*

Her frustration, her recognition of inevitable disaster came to a head on Saturday afternoon, when a local florist delivered a dozen red roses to her door. Dory looked at the bloodred blossoms, smelled their pungent fragrance as she read the florist's card. Across the top was the imprinted message, "Hope you're feeling better soon." The signature, written by a stranger's hand, said simply, "Scott."

Dory felt her heart breaking into pieces as she set the vase of flowers on the table. Crossing her hands over her chest, gathering handfuls of her knit shirt in her fists because she had nothing else to hold on to, she surrendered to sobs that began with a low wail from deep in her throat and then grew into spasms that shuddered through her entire body.

When she had worn herself out, she stared at the roses. Why couldn't they have been daisies or balloons or peppermint carnations, anything but bloodred roses? Scott had bought her teddy bears and sexy teddies, crazy mugs, cards that made her blush when she read them. He'd brought her a wooden pet slug refrigerator magnet from Seattle. He'd bought her salt water taffy and cotton candy and corn dogs and prime rib. He'd bought her bouquets of mixed flowers at supermarkets and potted plants at K-Mart. But he'd never sent her a dozen red roses.

Red roses. So formal. So predictable. So cliché. So uncharacteristic of their relationship, so contrary to the way they usually communicated.

She looked at the bouquet and thought, *Red roses. Oh Scott, is this what we've come to? How did we ever get from pet slugs for the refrigerator to bloodred roses?*

7

"A BABY?"

It occurred to Dory, as she surveyed the shocked faces of her father, mother, sister and brother, that the announcement of impending birth seemed to prompt a parroting response.

"A baby? Is that all you guys can come up with?" she asked. "Isn't anybody going to say, Dory, what wonderful news?"

Her father, in an uncharacteristic bout of inarticulateness, sputtered something that wasn't quite a word and shifted uncomfortably in the recliner where he sat as if on a throne. Her mother's face was so flushed she looked apoplectic. Hand on throat, she didn't even try to speak. Adelina was seated in a wing chair in a modeling school posture, displaying a beauty-contestant's poised aloofness, as though the entire distasteful situation had nothing to do with her.

Sergei, good old Sergei, looking every inch the eminently successful pioneering young surgeon, unfolded from the sofa, walked to Dory, embraced her and said, "So when's the big date?"

"The end of May or beginning of June," Dory said, giving her brother a grateful hug.

The judge paused while tamping down the tobacco he'd just scooped into his pipe. "That'll be cutting it a little close, won't it? How far along are you?"

Dory gave him a blank look. "I'm not sure I know what you mean. There's a timetable to these things."

Sergei laughed nervously, then said, "Dory, he was asking about the wedding. When are you and Scott tying the knot?"

Dory had anticipated the expectation, but she wasn't prepared for the terrible silence that awaited the burst of the bombshell she was about to drop. Her face grew hot, and she flicked her tongue over her lips before she threw back her head and said, "Scott and I aren't going to get married."

Her father slammed his pipe into the ash tray. "That gutless, son-of-a-bitching Gator!"

Dory set her mouth to respond to the outrageous slur, when her mother wheezed, "Dory, how could you? An illegitimate baby! I'll be cashiered out of the Guild." She paused, pondering the situation further, then said, "I'll never live it down."

"You helped organize the Tallahassee Symphony, Mother. You're an institution. They'll hardly wrest you from the string section for your grown daughter's indiscretion. Especially after the scandal with that violinist a couple of seasons ago."

"She was only with us that one season," Mrs. Karol said defensively.

Dory was too wound up to let the irrelevant issue drop. "At least I know who the father of my baby is. It was conceived in love. Your little protégé was so kinky for policemen she wasn't sure which officer on the night shift to point a finger at."

"Dory!" her mother said.

"That's enough of that kind of talk, young lady!" growled the judge. Then, for good measure, he added,

"A lot of good it does to know who the father is when the bum won't marry you."

"Father!" She spun to direct a scowl down her nose at him. "You know how it is with Scott and me."

"You're pregnant," he said bluntly. "I knew no good would come from your dating that damned Gator."

Dory rolled her eyes in exasperation. "This has nothing to do with ridiculous college rivalries." She exhaled wearily. "You *like* Scott and you know it."

"Liked," the judge harrumphed, stressing the past tense of the word. "But that was when I thought he had a backbone."

Adelina sprang from her chair and folded her arms across her chest, temporarily losing her modeling school cool. "I just hope the scholarship committee doesn't hear about this."

Dory turned to Sergei with a challenging scowl. "Well, big brother? What about you? What words of cheer do you have about the impending blessed event?"

At a loss for words, he said her name placatingly.

Dory looked from her father's face, red with fury; to her mother's, colored by humiliation; to her sister's, distorted by righteous indignation; to Sergei's, soft with sympathy. "I need some fresh air," she said, and scurried out the back door to the screened porch.

For several minutes she stood near the outer screen wall, staring at her mother's rose bushes, still in profuse bloom in late November. The red ones prodded her memory like a thorn through the brain. Scott. Maybe she should have waited until he was with her to tell her family. Or maybe it was better this way. She allowed herself a thin, ragged sigh. Or maybe there just wasn't any good way for a woman to tell her prim-and-proper family she's on the verge of single motherhood.

An ironic smile curved her mouth as she recalled Scott's prediction of her father's reaction. He'd known her father better than she did.

Weary, Dory flopped onto a wicker love seat, picked up one of the ruffle-edged pillows propped against the opposite arm and hugged it to her chest. In the far side of the house someone began playing the piano, not a melody, but chords and scales. Inevitably singing followed. Adelina, diligently going through her daily vocal exercises. Dory's mother was probably chording for her on the piano.

Closer to the porch, the sounds of cheering football crowds drifted through the door from the television in the den. The two noises merged into a queer but familiar cacophony. *The proud and the profane*, Dory thought acidly and wondered which was which.

The door opened, and Sergei stuck his head through tentatively. "Feel like some company?"

Good old Sergei. Dory patted the empty space next to her on the seat.

For a while, they didn't talk, just sat quietly listening to the sounds indigenous to the Karol household.

"Adelina's in good form," Dory commented idly.

"You wouldn't expect her to let a little thing like Thanksgiving interfere with her practice schedule, would you?"

"She has to stay ready," Dory said.

"For what?"

"The Met, of course."

"Or the next Miss Florida pageant, whichever comes first," Sergei quipped.

"That's tacky," Dory said, but she laughed. Very quickly, though, she sobered. "At least one of us turned out the way we were supposed to."

Sergei gave her a playful chuck on the arm. "Hey kiddo, maybe we didn't follow our prospective name-sakes, but you and I aren't exactly n'er-do-wells."

After a pause, Dory said, "Who would have thought it? How could two people progressive and freethinking enough to name their children after Isadora Duncan, Sergei Rachmaninoff and Adelina Patti be so . . . stodgy and traditional?"

"You threw them a real curve, Isadora."

"What now? Do I get the lecture on giving them some time? Letting them adjust?"

Sergei let the rhetorical questions pass without comment. A full minute passed before he said, "Dory?"

The heaviness of his tone made her look at his face.

He said, "I know you, the way you're always noble and like to see things through, but this is a biggie, Dory. If you want me to, I can arrange for you to see a friend of mine. It wouldn't be like a clinic, going in and out in an assembly line. He could take care of it very discreetly in his office."

"How very nice," Dory said, the words dripping with sarcasm. "And how very important to be discreet."

She sat very still, stinging from this final betrayal, staring straight ahead with unfocused eyes, knowing that if she moved, if she allowed herself to see or feel or hear anything she would lose the last shred of dignity and control. Sergei put his hand on her arm, and she jerked away from him. "Don't touch me, Sergei. Don't . . . touch . . . me."

"I was only trying to help."

Dory turned to him. "How could you? Remember Julius Caesar . . . 'Et tu, Brute?' That's exactly how I feel now. 'Et tu, Sergei?'"

"I was only trying to help," he repeated. "I didn't know how strongly you felt about it."

"It? Sergei, what do they teach you guys in med school? I thought the emphasis was on life, but I'm not so sure. First my doctor, and now you. *You*. Sergei! My favorite brother! How can you say 'it' that way, when you're referring to your niece or nephew?"

Sergei threw up his arms. "All right, Dory. I made a mistake. An error in judgment. Chop off my head, if you want; my heart was sincere. If you want this baby—and obviously you do, it's not just some sense of obligation you're feeling—then I'll be the best damned uncle a kid could ever want."

"You mean that, don't you?" Dory asked, turning tear-brightened eyes on his face.

Sergei put his arm across her shoulders and hugged her. "Of course I do. You're Isadora, with two left feet, and I'm Sergei with the tin ear. We have to stick together, kid."

"It's still too sad to be funny, isn't it?" Dory said. "Two overachievers feeling inadequate for not being born with the talents compatible with our imposing names."

Sergei shrugged, and chuckled. "There's still Adelina and the Met."

"Or the next Miss Florida pageant, whichever comes first."

They laughed, then sobered.

"They were pretty tough on you inside," Sergei said.

"Hypocrites! They wouldn't have been so outraged if Adelina had come up pregnant by that dilettante composer she was playing around with last year. I can just hear mother rhapsodizing about what beautiful music the child would create."

"You didn't think much of the young maestro, did you?"

"Give me credit for some taste. That pompous, pretentious boor? Going on and on about creativity in modern classical music—his compositions made 'Farmer in the Dell' sound like a work of creative genius."

"I've never known you to get so passionate over music."

"Music, hell! That Don Juan of progressive symphony made a grab for me in the kitchen."

Sergei produced a croak of laughter. "He what? He didn't!"

"While mother was in the living room dreaming about the perfect match between her youngest daughter and the maestro, the maestro was in the kitchen trying to seduce her first-born daughter. If that kid doesn't make it as a conductor, it won't be because he doesn't have quick hands."

"Lord, Dory. Did you tell Adelina?"

"Are you kidding? She'd never have spoken to me again. She's a genius. I figured she'd see through him sooner or later. Or, at the very least, get tired of his plodding melodies."

"Which was it?"

"She found him humming one of his melodies to a harpist in a private practice room. In a rather unorthodox position under the harp."

"You made that up."

"Only the part about the harp."

A silence trailed their light banter, growing long and heavy. "They'll come around," Sergei assured her. "Father's all bluster, and you know how mother is about babies."

"She's great with them in ten-minute stretches."

"She'll last at least twenty minutes with a grandchild."

"Even an illegitimate one?"

"Dory, when she holds that grandbaby in her arms and it nuzzles against her breast, she's not going to give a tinker's damn about pieces of paper and you know it."

Dory lifted her head from the crook of his elbow. "You're certainly poetic all of a sudden."

"I did my time in obstetrics, way back when. I observed a lot of bonding. Scott will come around, too."

"I'm so scared," she said. "Not for the baby, or being pregnant, but about Scott."

"I take it you'd say yes if he asked."

"If he asked for the right reason."

"A baby isn't reason enough?"

"It's not the right reason. I could make him marry me. I know I could. But I want him to want to marry me, not just go through the motions out of some sense of duty."

"The way you want this baby."

"The way I want this baby, *and* Scott." She let her neck fall back onto her brother's elbow and looked up at him. "You're a man, Sergei. Give me a male perspective—do I want too much?"

"My opinion doesn't count, Dory. You're my kid sister. I'd like to see you get everything you want, no matter what you set your heart on. Whether or not you're asking too much from Scott is something you're going to have to work out with him."

"Some help you are."

"Hey, I'm a surgeon, not a psychiatrist. If it's any consolation, though, I predict this baby will force the issue."

"That prediction didn't require clairvoyance."

"Want to talk about it some more?"

She shook her head. "I just spent the single most miserable three days of my life last weekend thinking about it. Talking it to death won't accomplish anything."

"Thank God," he said dryly.

"I'd like to talk about the baby," Dory said. "I did some reading. You know how when a baby's born, the parents count fingers and toes, just to make sure the baby's perfect?"

"Ridiculous, isn't it?"

"No. Not at all. It's sweet. Anyway I found out that my baby, my teeny-tiny baby, already has fingers and toes. It's only three inches long but it's already getting fingernails. Fingernails, Sergei. Think of that! What are you grinning at?"

"You. The way you go at life like a bulldozer. I've heard of women enchanted by being pregnant, but I've never heard of them making a big production over fingernails."

"We're talking about my child," Dory said intensely.

Sergei refused to pick up on her staid mood. "So let's talk about something really important to the Karol clan—what are you going to name this kid?"

"If it's a boy, I'm going to call him Refrigerator, after Refrigerator Perry, of course. He'll play for UF and be the first Gator in history to win the Lombardi Award. And if it's a girl . . ."

Sergei groaned. "I just realized I don't really want to know."

THE DAY AFTER Thanksgiving held little promise for Dory. She awoke nauseated and suffered a bout of morning sickness she felt certain would qualify her for the *Guinness Book of World Records*. *Must be the fingernails*, she thought, groaning into the cool, damp washcloth pressed over her face. Lord, but wouldn't her judgmental relatives love to see her like this.

By midmorning she'd recovered enough to shower and dress, if faded old jeans and an old FSU jersey could be considered dressed. She tried giving herself a pedicure, but the smell of the polish made her sick to her stomach, so she gave up on self-indulgence and turned on the television, flipping through the channels until she reached a talk show featuring people in three-way marriages. There was one group of two men and one woman, another of two women and one man. They were discussing the issues of fidelity, bisexuality and unconventional marriage structure. Dory clicked off the remote control with a savage stab. Weirdos! If and when she ever got Scott to the altar, she certainly wasn't magnanimous enough to share him with another woman. Or another man, for that matter.

She tried to read and was restless, tried to sleep and the phone rang. A wrong number. On impulse, she dialed Scott's home number, but got no answer. She might have worked, but she hadn't the enthusiasm. She might have gone to a movie, but she hadn't the energy.

She was not tired, for she had slept well. She was merely worn out, emotionally overextended from wanting too much, needing too much, loving too much. And, compounding her misery, her body was taut with the tension of deprivation, reminding her she was a week overdue for some quality bedroom activities. Scott withdrawal, that's what she was suffering.

When the doorbell rang, she toyed with the idea of ignoring it. It was probably Mrs. Viscount from downstairs, bringing her cake or pie or cookies. Mrs. Viscount always baked for special occasions. Dutifully, full of the righteousness of self-sacrifice, Dory sloughed from the couch and padded to the door. If Mrs. Viscount could be a generous soul, the least Dory could do was take some of the proffered cake and listen to a detailed account of the previous day's observances with Mrs. Viscount's children and grandchildren.

She opened the door so fully expecting Mrs. Viscount's visage that it took several seconds for her to recognize Scott. For an instant, she was stunned and motionless, and stood there just staring at him.

Scott shoved his suitcase past her and stepped inside. "I was going home, but the car wouldn't exit at Gainesville. The next thing I knew, I was on the Monroe Street off ramp."

Dory reacted like any mature red-blooded woman who'd been missing her lover and now discovered he was within reach. She leaped into his arms. Literally. Her arms clamped round his neck, anchoring her to him, and her legs went round his waist, compelling him to hold her, support her. Laughing, Scott threw his arms around her waist as he struggled for balance. Catching his footing, he walked to the edge of the sofa and fell back on it, carrying Dory with him. She was kissing him all over his face, his neck, behind his ears, blowing in his ear, nipping at his earlobes.

Still laughing delightedly, Scott fought to get his arms over hers so he could trap her face in his palms. "Gee, Dory, I was hoping you'd be glad to see me."

"What makes you think I'd be glad to see you?" Her face dipped to his, and she ran her tongue over his lips, coaxing them apart. Her kiss swallowed any answer he might have made as she plunged her tongue into his mouth, past his teeth, to tease the roof of his mouth. Her body pressed warmly into his as she lay atop him. Her legs had slid down until her ankles were locked around his. She slipped her toes under the bottom edge of his pants, pushed down on the top of his socks and contacted bare skin.

Scott groaned in response and thrust his fingers in her hair, molding them to her scalp, holding her head in place above him. Dory felt the hot firming of his loins against her pelvis and groaned back. She tore her mouth away from his and moved it to the hollow of his throat, drawing gently on his Adam's apple. Scott reached inside the bottom of her shirt to run his hands over her bare back. Dory gasped, and whispered, "Yes, touch me. Please. I need to know you're really here."

The beginning of an endearment rose in his throat, but Dory put her fingertips over his lips and shushed him. "Don't talk. You're here. That's enough."

He kissed her fingers, nipped the tips with his teeth, cupped her hand in his and flicked his tongue over her palm, tasting the salt of her skin.

With a sigh, Dory laid her cheek on his chest and listened to the quickened beat of his heart, content with the feel of his body under hers, the life sound of his blood rushing in response to their closeness. She found the scent of him arousing—the unique combination of after-shave, detergent, soap and man that was unique to this particular man. She wriggled against him in erotic, graceful movements. A rapturous groan started in his chest, near her ear, and rose to his throat, a sound that was uniquely his.

Scott. Her lover. Her friend. The father of her child. No matter what lay in their future, nothing could take away their past, the shared experiences, the love they'd made, the closeness they'd felt. She closed her eyes, just listening, feeling, breathing in his scent, cherishing the moment, collecting another sweet memory.

Scott grasped the tail of her shirt with one hand, ready to remove it. Dory stopped him. "No. Not yet. Let's keep our clothes on and make out for hours like teenagers."

"Dory, I'm horny as a teenager. Do you know how long it's been? How much I miss you when we're not together?"

"Indulge me," she said, swirling the tip of her tongue around the rim of his ear.

"You're serious, aren't you?" he said incredulously.

Her face hovered inches above his, her eyes locked with his. "It's just so special, your being here when I needed you so badly. Such a surprise. I want to enjoy this time, enjoy just being close to each other."

"We'll enjoy each other with our clothes off," he said desperately. "Trust me."

"Then let's compromise," she said, shoving his shirt up under his arms. She dropped her head to nuzzle her chin in his chest hair playfully, then puffed a gentle breeze of air through it, ruffling it. Moving slowly, she blew on the nipple of his right breast until it hardened, then flicked over it with her tongue before taking it in her mouth and sucking on it. Leaving it shiny with the dampness of her kiss, she did the same to his left nipple.

He said her name in appeal, and she raised her own shirt then lowered against him. Her pregnancy-ripened breasts compressed against his broad, hairy chest, and she sighed languidly. "Like teenagers," she whispered, smiling.

Scott ran his hands over her bare back. "Teenagers keep going out of curiosity. This is torture when you're accustomed to life beyond foreplay."

Dory raised her head to look down at him, and laughed softly. "Let me know when you're on the verge of losing control, and you can take me out for lunch."

"Lunch? At a time like this?"

"I'm suddenly starving."

He tightened his embrace, pulling her harder against him. "So am I, sweetheart."

"Really starving. For food. I haven't had anything all day."

"I haven't had any of you for weeks," he said, guiding her face to his, her lips over his own. His kiss was persistent, invasive, his hands equally so as they cupped and massaged her breasts. Dory folded her knees, drawing them up so that the throbbing area between her legs rested heavily over the hard flesh denied her by his pants. The sensual assault whipped her de-

sire for him into a maelstrom of longing, but she wanted
to prolong the sweetness of their time together, needed
to make this precious borrowed time memorable.

He insinuated his right hand between them to work
at the waistband of her jeans, succeeded in opening the
snap, then tugged at the zipper. The inevitable awkwardness and slight delay gave Dory time to regroup
her resolve. Dragging her mouth from his, she whim-
pered urgently, "Touch me, yes, touch me just a little,"
she said, and gasped as his finger found its way to the
place he knew from long experience she wanted him to
touch. She made one final movement against him, a
slight wriggle that left them both struggling for breath,
then gently guided his hand away from her. "Now," she
said, "take me to lunch."

"You're kidding," he said, taking in air in gulps.
"Please, Dory, tell me you're kidding."

"Like teenagers," she said, dropping a brief kiss on
his nose.

"We had a name for girls like you," he grumbled. "It
wasn't pretty."

"I'm not saying 'no'; I'm saying 'later.' There's a difference."

"I wish you'd explain it to the part of me you're sitting on."

"I'll move then," she said, and rolled off him. For a
split second she remained perched precariously on the
couch next to him, then grabbed for him as she tumbled backward to the floor.

Her eyes locked with his as she fell, and she recognized pure terror in the depths of them. She hardly felt
the ignominious thump of her backside on the floor, but

Scott was panicky as he knelt next to her. "Dory, are you hurt?"

"No," she said. "I bounced."

"Don't joke, Dory. You have to be careful."

Throwing her arms around him, she laughed from the sheer joy his concern brought to her. He hadn't mentioned the baby, but the concern was genuine, and transparent as glass.

"What is wrong with you?" he asked, exasperated. "What's so damned funny?"

"You are," she said in words tempered with love. "I fell off the couch, Scott, not a mountainside."

"I think sexual frustration is affecting your brain," he said. "Why don't you let me do something about it...?"

She shoved him away playfully. "Later, playboy. Now, if you'll just give me a boost up, I'm going to change clothes."

"I'll help," he volunteered.

She cast him a censorious look. "No way. You'll sit here on the sofa and wait for me very patiently. I won't be ten minutes."

"This is insanity," he called after her. She blithely ignored him.

"You said ten minutes," he complained, when she returned to the living room in slacks and a sweater. He made a show of checking his watch. "It's been fourteen."

"I took an extra few minutes to change the sheets," she said, and took pleasure in the expletive he produced in answer.

"WELL," HE SAID LATER, when they were settled in the car. "You seem to be calling the shots. Where to?"

The smile she turned on him was devastatingly seductive. "How about the Adams Street Commons?"

She continued taunting and teasing him all through lunch, pressing her calf against his under the table, brushing the top of his thigh with her fingertips when he wasn't expecting it, talking sexy to him with her eyes.

Finally, acutely exasperated, Scott said, "For crying out loud, Dory, what are you trying to do to me?"

"I'm seducing you, of course."

"You don't have to go to all this trouble. I was hot for you the minute you opened the door. Before. Hell, I'm always hot for you. Why play games?"

Another devastating smile, a bedroom come-on with her eyes, a sly smile. "The name of this game is foreplay." Shielded by the drop tail of the tablecloth, she ran the fingernail of her forefinger down the zipper of his pants and watched the shock play over his face. "I think I'm playing it well, don't you?"

"Dory!" he sputtered. "Do you want me to—"

"Oh, yes," she said, giving him an affectionate pat before lifting her hand to rest gracefully on the table. "Just as soon as possible."

"Which may be in a back alley or the back seat of my car if you keep this up."

"You've got more class than that," she said, rubbing his ankle with the toe of her shoe. "Especially when I just put fresh sheets on my bed." She picked up her sandwich, took a bite, chewed it with deliberate slowness, swallowed, licked her lips and purred a sensuous, "Um-m-m-m."

Scott was staring at her unabashedly. "The food is good here," she said. "Aren't you hungry?"

Scowling, Scott reached for his sandwich. "We've already established what I'm hungry for," he said, and bit into the sandwich savagely.

This was just like Dory, Scott was thinking. And while he was trying to be angry, he was too enchanted for anger. As exasperating as his frustration was, her ploys were working. She was expertly using anticipation as an aphrodisiac, and he wanted her as much at this moment as he ever had before. He never tired of her. She was so special; their time together was so special.

ON THE WAY HOME, Dory had him stop at a supermarket so she could dash in for some secret acquisition, insisting he stay in the car and wait for her. He sat there, drumming his fingers impatiently on the steering wheel, listening to the radio and feeling like a man in exile until she reemerged from the store carrying a large brown shopping bag that appeared empty.

He watched her approach the car, noting the grace in her movements, the feminine lilt of her step, the way her sweater draped over her breasts, the smile she flashed when she discovered him watching her. The warmth that had subsided while she was away gathered in his loins again. They were going back to her apartment where they'd be alone. Where she'd changed the sheets in anticipation of their lovemaking. Where he'd bury part of himself in her, and they'd become part of each other.

"Find what you were looking for?" he asked dryly as she somehow managed to bump her knee against his while fastening her seat belt.

"Um-hm," she replied. She looked like a svelte cat who'd swallowed a canary. When they reached the highway, she tugged at his shirt near the waistband of his pants until she'd worked the tail loose.

"Dory," he said. "I'm trying to drive."

Her hand spanned the flat of his stomach, just above his navel. "Go right ahead," she said. "I'm not stopping you." She didn't move her hand, didn't stroke or massage or move lower. She just left it there, letting the imprint of it burn its message into his flesh, then said, "You're awfully warm, Scott—you don't have a fever, do you?"

He chanced a glance at her and placed his right arm across her shoulders. "The only fever I've got is for you."

"I know," she said, nuzzling her forehead against his upper arm, "and I'm as anxious as you are."

As he turned into the parking area of her apartment complex, Dory withdrew her hand, then poked his shirt back into his waistband with her fingers, delving a bit deeper than was absolutely necessary. He tried to grab her hand before she pulled it away, but had to deal with the steering wheel instead as he maneuvered the car into a narrow space. By the time he'd switched off the engine and twisted to give her his full attention, she was sitting primly in the seat with the shopping bag balanced on her lap.

"Just wait until I get you inside," he grumbled, and reached for the door handle. They might as well have been total strangers as she preceded him up the sidewalk, carrying the shopping bag, gingerly holding the top closed with her fists. Scott deliberately hung back, letting a distance grow between them. "Your behind wiggles when you walk," he said.

Still clutching the bag, Dory stopped at her door, waiting for Scott to open it with his key. She stepped inside ahead of him and walked directly to the bedroom. Scott followed, but she turned and stopped him at the door. She had set aside the grocery bag, and now she put her arms around his neck and kissed him gently on the lips. But when Scott attempted to deepen the kiss, she drew away from him. "I need five minutes," she said.

"Dory!"

"Five minutes," she repeated, cradling his cheek in her palm. "Please, Scott. I'm looking forward to being with you, and I want it to be . . . special."

"But . . ."

"I want to get into something sexy."

Scott groaned reluctant acquiescence. "You have one hell of a way of winning an argument."

Dory smiled, kissed him on the cheek and playfully steered him through the door, then closed it.

"Five minutes," he called from the other side. "Not a second more."

Exactly five minutes later, Scott discovered that the door was locked. He jiggled the knob impatiently. "Dory!"

"Pick it," she said.

It was an easy lock to pick, requiring only the nose of a screwdriver or some similar flat blade. Unable to locate a screwdriver, Scott resorted to using a kitchen knife. "I should kick it in," he called through the wood, when the knife proved to be less than ideal for the job.

The lock chose that instant to yield, and he strode into the room with the stance of a man with a purpose.

"You wouldn't want to upset Old Lady Viscount, would you?" Scott followed the sound of Dory's soft voice to its source and froze. She was stretched out in the bed, covers up to her midriff, propped up on one elbow. She was wearing her sexiest satin baby dolls. When he looked at her, she patted the empty space next to her, where the covers were folded back invitingly. And on the pillow, his pillow, there was a single red rose with a ribbon bow tied on the stem.

The drapes were drawn, and lighted candles on the bedside table winked a gentle, fluctuating light into the twilight.

Several seconds ticked by before Scott began undressing slowly, self-conscious as she watched him with avid, curiously innocent carnal fascination, as though she hadn't seen him naked hundreds of times, touched him in all the private places he gradually unveiled for her. With an uncharacteristic stab of modesty, he left his briefs on, though his arousal was blatantly apparent beneath the thin fabric.

Dory rose to her knees and picked up the rose as he sank into a sitting position on the edge of the bed. She put her arms around him, pressing her satin-clad breasts against the broad expanse of his back, and offered the rose to him by tickling it under his nose. He raised his hands to capture hers and lifted one of her palms to his mouth to kiss it. She moved back, pulling him with her, and he twisted onto the bed, onto smooth, cool sheets still fresh with the ambrosial scent of fabric softener.

Shifting so that she was beside him, Dory traced his profile from forehead to chin with the petals of the rose, then drew imaginary patterns on his chest with it, finally teasing over his nipples with it as she looked down at him adoringly.

Scott caught her wrist, staying it, and locked his gaze with hers. Then, slowly, he reached up to cradle her face with his hands and gently coax it down to his.

"My behind doesn't wiggle when I walk," she whispered.

"It wiggles beautifully," he said. "I love the way it wiggles." Their lips touched tentatively, then conformed to each other with graceful ease.

Time stood still for them in the candle-lit bedroom as they loved each other tenderly and well. Afternoon stretched into evening, evening into dead of night, but they were too lost in each other to pay homage to a clock. The candles burned on, casting dancing light on the ceiling until, one by one, they blinked out with a final puff of smoke. Scott and Dory caressed one way and then another, making love in ways both old and new to them, discovering new expressions of their feelings, rediscovering old ones. In between, they cuddled and dozed, sleeping with limbs entwined.

At one point Scott awoke to find Dory gone. He found her in the bathroom, drawing bath water. The scent of her bath oil hung in the steamy fog lifting from the tub, and Scott breathed it in, feeling surrounded by Dory even as he admired her nude body from across the small room.

She smiled at him as she stepped into the tub. He waited until she was settled, then asked, "Mind some company?"

"Not in the least."

He lowered himself behind her, straddling her hips with his legs, which he kept bent at the knee. His arms encircled her waist. Dory relaxed her shoulders against his chest, and tilted her head back against his sternum. His chin lighted on the top of her head, and she felt his breath flutter through her hair. Her breasts floated just above his muscular forearms in the warm fragrant water; his penis, firming in testament to her effect on him, pressed into the flesh just below the small of her back. She thought idly that she could spend the rest of her life there with him and be utterly content.

For several minutes silence swirled round them, soothing as the bathwater. Then Dory murmured, "It's good between us, isn't it?"

"It's better than good."

The unsettling knowledge of inevitable change molested the prolonged silence that followed this exchange.

"There's more than this between us, isn't there?" Dory said. "More than strong sexual chemistry."

"We've been making love since early afternoon, Dory. Sex was only part of what was going on between us." He tightened his arms around her, and raised them slightly, lifting her breasts. "What we're both feeling now is not wholly sexual. We're as close as any two human beings can be. Even when I'm in Gainesville missing you, wishing you weren't so far away, I feel close to you."

"I'm glad. I feel the same way when we're apart. Like we're not completely apart as long as I can keep you close in my mind."

Her languid sigh was the only imperfection in another prolonged silence. Then she said, "I think it happened here. That time I got in the shower with you." Her laugh was whisper soft. "The floor was flooded, remember?"

His chest moved under her as he chuckled. "I remember." Half a minute later, he asked, "Why do you think that's when . . . ?"

"Instinct. The timing's right. And the water might have . . ." She struggled over the right words. When he'd shown up so unexpectedly, she hadn't meant to talk about the baby unless he brought up the topic. She drew in a deep breath, and began the sentence over. It came out in a rush of words. "The water might have washed away the cream."

"All those times," Scott said. "We were so careful for so long. And something as simple as bathwater . . ."

It wasn't the reply she would have wanted him to make, not the attitude she would have liked for him to have. "I hope it *was* that day," she said intensely. "I hope that *is* when it happened. It was . . . memorable. When I think about it, I remember what a surprise it was, what a sweet surprise. Like your showing up today."

"I couldn't stay away. Especially after Sergei called."

She raised her head and twisted to look at his face questioningly. "Sergei called you?"

"He said he thought you could use a friend."

"Good old Sergei."

"I would have come anyway. I was missing you too much to wait to see you." He dropped a kiss on her temple. "Incidentally I've been so . . . *distracted* since I got here, I haven't had time to tell you. Dean Baxter's open house is Friday after next. Do you think . . . if you took half a day off...you'd feel up to coming to Gainesville for it? Mike and Susan want to get together, too. Maybe we could go to dinner with them afterwards."

"Sounds great." So *normal*.

"Then you'll come?"

"I'll buy a new dress for it. Something festive and sexy as all get-out."

He gave her a friendly squeeze. "I'll look forward to seeing it. Now—tell me about your family. How bad was it?"

"How bad did Sergei tell you it was?"

"He didn't go into details."

"You were right about father's reaction. You're not his favorite person right now."

"I was never his favorite person."

"Mother's considering resigning from the Guild, and Adelina was flapping around hysterically about the scholarship committee revoking her scholarship."

"Would they do that?"

Dory gave him a companionable elbow jab in the ribs. "Get serious. Revoke a talent scholarship on the grounds of a pregnant older sister? Pregnancy's not a felony, you know. I'm not Princess Di or Lady Sarah, and as much as I love you, you're not a prince, literally. This is just a cozy little family baby, not a front-page event."

They were quiet a few minutes, serious, thoughtful, before Dory observed, "The water's getting cold."

"Why don't you add some fresh hot?"

"I don't think so. If we stay in too long, we'll shrivel."

She moved to get up, but he anchored her in front of him by tightening his arms. "Don't pull away from me."

"I'm not pulling away. Come on. It's late. We'll go back to bed. Together." She sprang the lever that opened the drain.

Scott stood up with a whoosh of water, and helped Dory up. "Careful. The tub's slippery."

They dried on the bath blanket Dory kept for Scott's visits. Scott, with the large towel over his shoulders, guided Dory in the terry cocoon with him and held her close to him. When he kissed her briefly on the lips, she responded by flinging her arms around his neck and clinging to him with an intense, desperate strength. "I'm scared," she said. "Oh, Scott, I'm so scared."

"Not for the baby?"

She shook her head against his shoulder. "No. For us. For what we have. We have so much—so very much to lose."

Smoothing her hair with his fingertips, he kissed the top of her head and exhaled a heavy, masculine sigh. "I'm as scared as you are, Dory."

Their lovemaking, when they returned to the bed, was gentle and unhurried and poignantly bittersweet. In the mellow afterglow of it, they slept until nearly noon.

DORY FOUND THE ROSE, petals wilted and stem bent, when she started pulling the sheets straight to make the bed. She cradled it in her palms like a precious artifact. Seeing what she was holding, Scott said, "Oh, too bad. We should have been more careful. Here, I'll throw it away."

"No," Dory said, shielding it when he reached for it. Then, slightly embarrassed, she confessed, "I want to save it. I'll press it in a book."

Scott kissed her forehead. "There's something of a romantic in you."

"Um-hm," she agreed absently, thinking, *And the next time you send me red roses, they'll mean something.*

8

DORY TRIED ON half a dozen dresses before it dawned on her that it was no coincidence that every one of the dresses in her normal size was too snug for her, straining across her breasts and nipping into her waist. She reacted to the proof of her body's changes with surprise, then irritation, then fascination. Up to the point when she found the sixth dress she'd picked out didn't fit, her pregnancy had been more a matter of mind than of body. Now it was as physical as emotional.

She was pregnant. She was a pregnant woman. The idea of it boggled her mind anew. Stripped to her slip and bra, she studied her reflection in the dressing room mirror, scrupulously surveying the fullness of her breasts and new thickness of her middle. She spread her hand over her abdomen, still only minutely distended, and pressed gently, searching with touch for the life within. She found only a tiny, hard mass that she felt inside rather than with her fingers. The secret still belonged to her and those with whom she chose to share it, but it was a secret so imposing, so important, so awesome that the knowledge of it filled her from head to toe and side to side. Her body was swelling with it. And her baby, that solid little lump within her, had never seemed more real to her.

After an exhaustive search, she found a party dress with loosely fitted princess lines. It was a departure from the styles she usually wore, but the bright crimson hue and sheen of the heavy taffeta, tempered by ivory lace at the neck and sleeves, made it appropriate for a holiday open house.

DORY LAUGHED DELIGHTEDLY in response to the lusty wolf whistle Scott produced when she made her grand entrance to his living room wearing the red dress. "Do you really like it?" she asked. "I can't make up my mind. I feel a little like Santa Claus's wife."

Scott walked over to put his arms around her. "You're much younger than Mrs. Claus." He kissed her briefly on the lips, then cradled her chin with his fingers and studied her face. "You're very sexy in red. I may keep you here and hang you on my tree."

"And what would you do with me when you took the tree down on New Year's Day?" she asked. A few months earlier she wouldn't have given his flirtatious comment a second thought, except to feel a preening satisfaction in Scott's wanting her near. Now she noticed the flip sides of his endearments, the subtle reminders of the time and distance restrictions on their relationship.

"Wrap you in tissue and toss you in the attic with the rest of the ornaments," he teased.

It wasn't what Dory wanted, or needed, to hear. She forced a smile that masked a hurting heart, and said, "Then maybe you'd better take me to the open house instead. The attic's too stuffy for me."

Business school dean Reginald Hargrove had married the heiress to a very old and venerable fortune, and the couple lived in a very old and venerable mansion near the university. The house, which was charming and tastefully decorated with understated elegance at any time of the year, was especially charming at Christmas. Boughs of fresh evergreen, anchored by wide red ribbons, flanked the banisters and mantel. Sprigs of holly dotted the centerpieces and circled the bases of chunky red bayberry candles.

The air-conditioning was turned full force to compensate for the crowd and the heat of an oak fire in the huge fireplace, where hot apple cider spiced with cinnamon, cloves and dried citrus rinds simmered in a brass cauldron, adding to the essence of Christmas that hung in the air. The cider was tended by a maid in a black uniform and starched white apron who ladeled it into ironstone mugs decorated with a Christmas motif.

The dean's wife, Chelsey, wearing a floor-length tapestry skirt and a hand-embroidered linen blouse with mutton-leg sleeves, greeted them at the door, then circulated with them through the crowd until one of Scott's fellow accounting professors hailed them with a wave of the hand and struck up a lively conversation. Then she graciously excused herself to go back to the door and greet still other guests.

Gradually the crowd segregated into male and female camps. When the dean buttonholed Scott to get his input regarding possible ways of reducing spending within the department to accommodate a budget cut in the coming year, his wife hooked her wrist around Dory's elbow. Rolling her eyes, she said, "Men! They'll be discussing that proposed budget cut all evening."

She steered Dory to a cluster of women, many of whom Dory remembered from previous open houses. Amy Reynolds, the flaxen-haired beauty who'd been the belle of the open house two years earlier on the eve of her wedding to a finance professor, was in the full bloom of pregnancy. She was discussing Lamaze classes with Eleanor Triffle, the mother of four and an avowed advocate of natural childbirth.

Mary Ellen Wycliff, who ran a trendy boutique in the strip of shops just off-campus and taught a seminar course in small business management, interjected a comment about the fashionable maternity clothes now available, then turned to Dory. "Aren't you Scott Rowland's significant other?"

"I beg your pardon?" Dory said.

"Aren't you with Scott Rowland? We met last year."

"Yes. Of course. I remember you. And I'm with Scott. But what was the term you used?"

Mary Ellen laughed. "Oh—you mean *significant other*? I wasn't trying to be insulting. You must not have seen the memo about the open house. It said that all faculty members, spouses and significant others were invited. It's sort of a catch phrase around the campus. A sign of the times, I guess. Sure beats *main squeeze*."

"It certainly does that," Dory agreed. So now there was a name for what she was to Scott. She was his significant other. A year ago she would have laughed at the nomenclature. This year she found it chafing.

"Are you still living in Tallahassee?" Mary Ellen asked. Dory nodded, and the woman shook her head. "That must make it difficult for the two of you."

"We do a lot of driving," Dory said drolly.

Suddenly the *House Beautiful* room was too warm, too fragrant, too crowded. Dory fought a bout of light-headedness with sheer strength of will, but she must have wobbled slightly, because Mary Ellen asked, "Are you all right? You look a little flushed."

"It's a little warm in here," Dory said. "I think I'll see if I can find a glass of ice water in the kitchen."

Scott found her there a few minutes later, seated at the table under the welcome draft of an air-conditioning vent. "Dory?" he said, stopping next to her. "I looked over and you were gone."

"It was warm, and I got thirsty for something cold. Since I didn't want champagne punch . . ." She picked up the goblet of water from the table and tilted it back and forth, rattling the ice cubes. "If you'll refill this for me, we can get back to the party. There's a dispenser in the corner."

A uniformed maid who'd been rinsing dishes at the sink and stacking them into a dishwasher turned and took the glass from Scott's hand. "I'll get that for you," she said, and carried it to the dispenser. The water inside the large glass bottle made a liquid slurping sound as she refilled the glass at the push-button dispenser. "Here you go," she said, giving it back to Dory with a smile.

Dory thanked her and rose, wincing slightly when she reached her full height. "Are you sure you're okay?" Scott asked.

"I shouldn't have worn high heels," she answered, then added in a confidential whisper, "My ankles are a little swollen."

The hardening of his features at the nebulous reference to her pregnancy saddened her. *Why can't you be happy with me?* she thought frantically, frustrated because she couldn't say it aloud. Aloud, it would be an accusation.

THE DAY AFTER the open house, they drove fifteen miles south of Gainesville to Micanopy, a turn-of-the-century town just up the road from Marjorie Kinnan Rawling's Cross Creek estate. Micanopy had never been big, and now consisted primarily of a palatial old Southern home, the Herlong Mansion, which had been converted into a bed and breakfast, and a row of vintage wooden buildings that now housed antique, crafts and specialty shops.

Scott and Dory went browsing through the shops about twice a year, always in a spirit of fun. It was in Micanopy, at the wood-carver's store, that Dory had bought Scott a carved wooden whistle that produced a sound like an old-fashioned steam whistle on a locomotive, because he'd been more excited over it than the children to whom the storekeeper was showing it.

At the hodge-podge, old-but-not-necessarily-antique store, Scott had bought Dory a ceramic bud vase shaped like Bugs Bunny. For the next two weeks, they'd sent silly cards to each other's office with, "What's up, Doc?" written inside. Dory had a homemade carrot cake waiting for Scott the next time he came to Tallahassee, and in appreciation, he took her shopping for the half-carat diamond stud earrings she'd always wanted.

She was wearing the earrings today, and unconsciously reached up to touch the smooth surface of one of the diamonds. "Remember the day we bought my Bugs Bunny vase?" she asked.

A smile broke on Scott's face as he nodded. "Maybe we'll find a companion piece for it today."

Dory chuckled. "Elmer Fudd?"

"Or the Tasmanian Devil."

"Or the abominable snowman—I'll hug him and kiss him and call him 'George.'"

"Something's going on at the mansion," Scott said. At his abrupt change of mood, Dory followed his gaze through the windshield. Ahead of them, traffic had ground to a near halt as drivers jockeyed for parking spaces on either side of the road that ran past the stately old mansion. A crowd was gathering on the wide front lawn.

The men were wearing coats and ties, and the women were in silk suits or dresses trimmed in lace. "Looks like a party," Dory said.

"Umm," Scott agreed. He eased the car past the mansion to park at the far end of the shops beyond, and they started their shopping expedition.

A wooden cradle with the heart carved out of the headboard seemed to leap out at Dory as they meandered through the second antique shop. She stopped and stared, imagining it lined with a tiny mattress, and a pink or blue comforter. Leaning over, she gave it a gentle nudge and set it rocking on the curved ends.

Scott, who'd been riffling through a display of old postcards, found her watching the cradle with a gentle smile on her face and soft dreams dancing in her eyes. His body constricted at the sight of her. His throat grew tight, and his chest felt as though a metal clamp was tightening around it.

She noticed him, looked up and smiled. "It's beautiful, isn't it?"

It felt to him as though the floor was turning to jelly under his feet. He managed a nod of agreement, but Dory didn't seem to notice his discomfort.

"I just realized I haven't given a single thought to a nursery, beyond the thought that I'll need one."

He still didn't reply; she still didn't seem to notice.

"I suppose it's too soon to actually buy—" Finally noticing his reticence, she laughed nervously. "Of course it's too soon. I haven't even thought about a color scheme."

The shopkeeper approached them tentatively and asked, "Is there anything I can help you find?"

"I was admiring this cradle," Dory said, running her fingertips over the smooth rim of the headboard. "How old is it?"

"About fifty years," the shopkeeper replied. "It's only halfway to becoming a genuine antique."

"It's lovely," Dory said.

"Yes. And handmade. It's a shame it's not more practical."

"Practical?"

"Well, everyone who looks at it points out that it's not a standard size, so it would require a special mattress and bumper pads. And the sides aren't high enough, so once the baby started pulling up, they'd have to move it to a standard crib, anyway."

"What age would that be?"

The woman shrugged. "Four months? Seven months? It's been so long since mine were that tiny. I don't remember exactly when they start pulling up."

Dory rocked the crib with a caring touch. "When the baby outgrew it, you could leave it in the nursery and put dolls or teddy bears or other stuffed animals in it."

The saleswoman gave Dory a warm smile. "Shopping for antiques and old things is a matter of the heart, like falling in love, isn't it? I could point out that this cradle is too low, and you'd have to bend over to pick up the baby and it wouldn't make a bit of difference to you, would it?"

Dory returned the smile. "No. It would still be just as beautiful." *And I would still look at it and see my baby sleeping in it.* After a beat, she laughed softly. "I'm not putting myself in a very strong bargaining position, am I?"

"It doesn't matter here," the woman replied. "I post my prices. I try to make them fair, but I don't 'bargain.' So your secret's safe with me. I wouldn't jack up a price because I know you want it."

Dory bent to read the price tag on the cradle and cringed.

"It *is* handmade," the shopkeeper said defensively.

"We were just browsing anyway," Scott said. Dory gave him an odd look, and he cocked an eyebrow at her. "Weren't we?"

"Yes," she said, unconvincingly. "Yes, we were only looking."

"If you see anything else you like and want to ask questions, I'll be at the register," the shopkeeper said.

When she was out of earshot, Scott turned to Dory. "You weren't seriously considering buying it, were you?"

"I don't know. Something about it . . . it's so pretty." She traced the inside of the carved heart with her forefinger. "I can . . . Scott, I can feel the love that went into making it."

"But the shopkeeper says it's impractical."

"Practicality isn't everything. As she said, buying antiques is like falling in love. It's a matter of the heart."

"Three hundred dollars is a lot of heart."

With one last, lingering look at the cradle, Dory shrugged and turned away. "You're probably right."

Scott stretched an arm across her shoulders and gave her a consoling hug. "Come on. There's a postcard I want you to see."

A few minutes later they were at the needlecraft shop, where needlepoint ornaments adorned an eight-foot Christmas tree, and potpourri candles disseminated the scent of evergreen and spice into the air. A family of plush teddy bears in varying sizes were scattered under the tree, all painstakingly dressed in turn-of-the-century costumes.

In another corner a basket had been draped with brown fabric to make it appear to be a hole in the ground, and around it were dozens and dozens of rabbits. Large, medium and small, black, white, tan or brown, all with floppy ears lined in pink satin, each rabbit had a distinct face and personality. Dory picked up a medium-sized tan rabbit wearing denim coveralls with a calico patch on the seat. It had ears that reached to its knees, tiny freckles on its face and an embroidered smile so lopsided and guileless that it defied one not to smile back at it. It also had a fifty-five dollar price tag.

"That's highway robbery," Scott said.

"It's handmade," Dory said, reading the carrot-shaped tag dangling from the rabbit's neck. "Look. Each one is individualized by the artist."

"It's still highway robbery."

Dory hugged the rabbit to her bosom. "I'll hug him, and kiss him, and call him 'George,'" she teased.

"You can't be serious. We're supposed to be shopping for Christmas presents."

"It will be a Christmas present."

"Rabbits aren't really up Adelina's alley," Scott said. "She'd go for the teddy in the lamé evening gown."

"It's not for Adelina. It's for the baby."

"The b—"

Dory scowled at him. "What's wrong, Mr. Accountant? Can't you say it? It's just two syllables. Ba-by."

"Dory, be reasonable," Scott said, fighting to keep his voice low so that the other shoppers in the store wouldn't overhear.

"I don't feel like being reasonable," Dory whispered back. "I don't have to be reasonable. I'm pregnant. Mothers are authorized a little human sentiment. You looked at that cradle and saw nothing but wood. I saw a baby tucked in there, sleeping peaceably."

She shoved the rabbit under his nose. "You look at this rabbit and see a fifty-five dollar rip-off, but I see tiny arms hugging it, and little hands dragging it along by the ears. I see a child and a rabbit tucked under the covers together."

Drawing the toy back to her chest, she stroked its ears and sighed sadly. "Yes, Scott, I'm going to buy George here for my baby. Our baby. But I'm not going to wrap it. I'm going to put it on the headboard of my bed so I can keep it company until the baby gets here. And I'll feel even closer to the baby when I'm hugging it or talking to it."

She choked back a sob. "I've got to talk to someone, Scott. I'm all alone now, because my best friend in the whole wide world insists on sticking his head in the sand and pretending the baby doesn't exist."

"Dory. God, Dory..." He reached for her, but she spun away from him and dashed toward the cash register. He caught up with her as she joined the line of customers with purchases, and said, "I'm sorry." The stubborn set of her shoulders and harsh compression of her lips betrayed the strong emotions she was holding in check.

Scott exhaled defeatedly. "I'm sorry, Dory. Let me . . . why don't you let me buy it? For . . ." He still couldn't say it.

Dory pivoted slightly, so that her back was to him, still holding the rabbit against her chest protectively. "It's . . . I want to buy it," she said. "It's . . . personal."

"All right, if that's the way you want it," he said, acknowledging and bowing to her stubbornness, and the fierce independence that was as much a part of her as her hair or nose or fingers or toes. "I'll be at the bookstore if you need me."

Keeping her back to him, she nodded. He wanted to touch her, but was afraid they'd both lose control of the volatile situation if he did. So instead of putting his hands on her shoulders, he thrust them in his pockets. He shouldered the door open, setting off a serenade of sleigh bells, and stalked to the bookstore.

Strands of tinsel lining the windows and a token shelf of Christmas books were the only consolations the bookstore paid to the holiday season. Scott went to the maritime history section and scanned the titles without paying particular attention to them. Five, ten, fifteen minutes passed, and still Dory hadn't joined him.

Finally, worried, he gave the shopkeeper a half-hearted shrug that told him he hadn't found anything and went to find Dory. She was standing with several other shoppers at the end of the sidewalk, watching whatever was going on at the mansion. He walked over to stand behind her and looked over her shoulder.

On the porch of the mansion, a couple in formal Victorian wedding attire stood facing a minister in black robes and sashes. Their attendants fanned out along the porch like bright flower petals, and the wedding guests spilled across the lawn like an overturned basket of flowers.

Scott slid his arms around Dory's waist, and sighed involuntarily when she leaned against his chest. Almost as though in celebration of their touching, the trio of Renaissance musicians on the edge of the mansion porch broke out in strains of Mendelssohn. Scott pulled one arm from around Dory to use his thumb to wipe a tear from her cheek. She smiled and twisted her head so she could see him. "Weddings are always so sentimental."

A woman standing nearby raised a tissue to her nose and blotted. "You said it. I always cry, even if I don't know the couple."

"It's so romantic," observed another onlooker to her companion. "The mansion, the trees, the music."

Scott kissed Dory's hair where it covered her ear. "Ice cream, or home?"

"Ice cream," Dory said, and they walked together to the ice cream parlor.

They didn't talk much for the rest of the afternoon and through dinner, and when they did, it was not about the confrontation in the needlework shop. They didn't talk about *that* until late in the night. They'd showered separately and Dory, pleading exhaustion, had refused Scott's overtures of lovemaking, although she hadn't protested when he put his arm under her neck, and had cuddled against him the way she normally did when they slept together.

It wasn't until he heard her breathing slow to near sleep that he found the courage to speak out. He began with her name, and she snuggled closer to him and murmured a sensuous, "Hmm?"

"Today," he said, "in Micanopy...when you were watching the wedding...were you—you were wishing it could be you, weren't you?"

The gravity with which he asked the question compelled Dory to wakefulness. Her eyes snapped open to the muted darkness of the bedroom. "Everyone wishes that at a wedding," she said. "It's all part of the beauty and emotionality of the event. It's only temporary."

"I've never wished it at a wedding. I've never looked at a groom and wished it was me standing up there."

"All right, Scott. I concede the point. I should have said every *woman* at a wedding—and that means the littlest girl to the most wrinkled old crone—dreams of being a beautiful bride. It's like going to the ballet and dreaming of being a prima ballerina."

"But today was different, wasn't it? Because..."

"Because I'm pregnant?"

Scott was too quiet. With a sigh of exasperation, Dory pulled herself to a sitting position, bracing herself with her elbows. "I've heard some pregnant pauses in my life, but that is about the most pregnant," she said. "You might as well get up and turn on the light if we're going to have a knock-down, drag-out fight."

While he was up, she stuffed her pillow against the headboard and resettled against it. Scott came back to bed, and sat down on the edge with one knee crooked on the bed and the opposite foot planted firmly on the floor. He lifted Dory's hands in his. "You want to get married, don't you?"

"You're challenging me," she said.

"I asked you a question."

"All the words were there, but the arrangement and sentiment were wrong."

"What the hell is that supposed to mean."

Dory couldn't help smiling at his dismay. Poor baby! He was so torn between what he was feeling and what he thought he ought to be feeling. She slid her right hand out from under his to brush the hair from his forehead. "It means that you asked me if I wanted to get married, but you didn't ask me to marry you."

"You're playing with words."

"No," she said. "The questions are quite different. One is a general, philosophical question, and the other is very personal."

"I saw the look in your eyes," he said.

"We'd just had a fight. I was vulnerable. And the wedding on the porch was very romantic. It was easy to get caught up in the romanticism of it."

"You'd like to get married," he challenged.

She refused to give him an easy out. "Yes, Scott," she admitted. "On one level I'd like to get married." She closed her eyes, squeezing the lids tightly, then opened them again. "But not to someone who looks at a wedding and thinks what a poor schnook the bridegroom is."

"I didn't say..."

"Not tonight, in so many words. But Scott, you've never made a secret of your scorn for marriage."

He poised his mouth to speak, but she shook her head. "No, don't interrupt me. I know you, Scott. In some ways, I probably know you better than you know yourself. Don't you think I know that when you look at a wedding couple, you're seeing your parents, and projecting all their unhappiness on the bride and groom?"

"My parents?"

"Of course. The only marriages you've been intimately privy to were your father's and your mother's. Their marriage to each other ended with your mother hurt and bitter. She married on the rebound, and the second marriage didn't last five years and left her more bitter than ever. And your father's second marriage has been an utter disaster for over twenty years. You don't mention him without mentioning how henpecked he is. You couldn't walk away from that environment anticipating entering into a mutually fulfilling, caring relationship. I don't think you've ever stopped to consider that such relationships exist, not even since we've been playing house."

"Our relationship works so well because we aren't together often enough to get on each other's nerves."

"Damn it, Scott! Don't you ever wonder what it would be like without the long, dry spells between visits? Don't you ever flop around in bed wishing Tallahassee wasn't so damned far away? Don't you ever have nights when you can't get to sleep and wish you had someone to talk to in the middle of the night?"

Scott exhaled a sigh. "You know I do, Dory. But . . ."

"Yes, Scott. I know you miss me and flop around in bed wishing I wasn't so far away, but you don't want to risk spoiling what we've got. You don't want us getting on each other's nerves or resenting each other. You don't want to have to answer to anyone when you want to work late or stay up half the night grading papers, and you don't want us sniping at each other over picayune issues."

"I thought you agreed with me," he said intensely. "I thought you were so tied up in your career that you felt the same way, wanted the same freedoms. I thought you thought what we had was as perfect as I did, because you didn't want any of those things, either."

Dory burst into tears, and threw her arms around his neck. "Oh, Scott, I don't. I mean, at least I never have. And I certainly didn't want a baby... at least, I didn't plan a baby right now. But I feel so alone in this. Every time I mention the baby, you freeze up on me. I want us to share this. It doesn't have to be every day. I just want to be able to tell you little things about the baby that no one else would care about and know that you care."

He nudged her head back and wiped the tears from her cheeks with his thumbs. His hands cradled her face as he spoke. "My caring for you has never been at issue, Dory. You know I care. I care for you so much the intensity of it terrifies me."

"Then why can't you care about our baby, too? That's the issue here. Not marriage. Not a piece of paper, but a baby, a tiny human being that's living inside me. It's part of you, Scott, just as it's part of me. That's one of the reasons I love it so much."

Scott's voice cracked with emotion as she nuzzled her face against his chest, clinging to him. "I care about the baby, Dory. When Mike said you weren't feeling well and I thought something might be wrong, I was frantic."

"You don't talk about it," Dory said. "You can't even say it. You can't say, 'baby.' I feel like you're trying to ignore it out of existence."

"I just keep asking why," he said. "Why now? Why us, when so many people want babies and can't have them. Why did it have to happen to us, when everything was so perfect?"

Dory raised her head and sniffed. "I met a woman at McDonald's," she said. "She had a beautiful little girl, and she wants to have another baby, but she's also had some miscarriages. I told her I hoped she did get pregnant again and have another baby, and you know what she said?"

He looked at her expectantly, waiting for her answer.

"She said, 'If it's meant to be, it will be.' I can't help feeling that way about our baby, Scott. It was a surprise to us, but we're not the power in charge of life. This child was simply meant to be. God gave it to us, and we have no right to shake a finger at Him and complain about bad timing."

"I'm not doing that. I'm...really...not...doing that."

"Aren't you? You keep talking about us, and what this'll do for us. Don't you think about the baby—our baby—at all? Don't you wonder what it'll look like, and whether it's a girl or a boy?"

"I haven't gotten that far yet," he admitted. "I can't get past the fear, Dory. Everything's changing. I don't want to lose you."

"You're not going to lose me, Scott, if—"

"I'm already losing part of you. You canceled a weekend, and that's never happened before."

"That was only because—"

"And you're changing, Dory. You've never been able to take an aspirin without a quart of water to wash it down, and now you're taking horse pills."

"Just vitamins. That's all."

"And you—I don't know you sometimes. You're so emotional, and you're holding back from me. There's an awkwardness between us that terrifies me. We've always been able to talk. Always. And now there's this terrible tension."

She caressed his cheeks in her palms. "I can't help the emotionality. I hate crying. I hate wimpy women who cry. But it's hormonal. And the only reason I'm holding back from you is that you don't want to hear what I have to say. Every time I bring up the baby you play turtle or ostrich on me. It's obvious you don't want to discuss it, and yet it's a big part of my life now. I have to think about it, because pregnancy is happening to me, to my body, and the baby will be sharing my life. If you want for us to go on sharing our lives, you're going to have to make a place for our baby, because I'm not going to be a solo act anymore."

She was crying again, being just as wimpy and sappy as any lily-livered female she'd ever scoffed at. Scott stretched out on the bed and pulled her into his arms. He kissed the top of her head and stroked her hair. "It tears me apart inside when you cry. And it scares me, because you're always so tough and strong and independent. I can't lose you. I won't. I didn't realize I was closing you out."

"Just share it with me," she said.

"What?" he asked. "Be specific. What to you want to share with me right this minute?"

"A miracle," she said. "The awe and wonder of it all."

"Tell me."

Dory sighed. "We keep asking why it happened to us, yet when you look at the reproductive process, conception itself is a miracle."

His right arm was around her, but she reached for his left hand and guided it, palm down, to her abdomen. "Think of it, Scott. One microscopic sperm reaches and joins with one microscopic egg. Even when you do everything just as nature intended, it's still a miracle that they find each other and combine to start a chain reaction of splitting and multiplying cells that eventually grow into a human being."

"The mug didn't lie—I really am a super stud."

Dory twisted her head and nipped a stretch of his chest muscle with her teeth and giggled when he jumped in surprise. "That's what I like to hear. Pride."

She pushed up on one elbow to look down at his face. "Oh, Scott, I want you to be proud. I am. Without even meaning to, we've done something wonderful."

There was a moment of golden, blissful silence, when the absence of tension between them was as significant as the oppressive tension had been earlier, a moment of tranquillity in the turbulent sea of change threatening to overwhelm them. Scott and Dory were content simply to lie close together and enjoy it.

Typically it was Dory who spoke first. "I'm getting fat."

Scott chuckled. "I wasn't going to mention it."

She gave his chest a playful slug with her fist. "I'm serious. I'm not officially showing, and I don't think I've gained pounds, but I had to buy a dress without a waistline, because every dress I tried on was too tight."

Hoping he would respond in some way, say something, make a joke, tease her about getting fat, she paused. Scott seemed content with the silence. She said, cautiously, "When your body starts changing on the outside, it makes you more aware of what's happening inside. It makes it more real."

Scott cleared his throat, as though he had a husk on it, but still didn't say anything.

"I'm beginning to want to tell people," Dory said. "Last night at the open house—"

"I saw you with Amy. I could tell you wanted to talk about babies." He folded his arm across his eyes. He sounded miserable. "I could read your mind, Dory." He lifted his arm and looked down at her face. "That's why you ran and hid in the kitchen, isn't it? You wanted to be a part of it and you couldn't."

"It was hot and stuffy in that room, and I was wearing those stupid high heels. I just needed a drink of water."

"You were about to say you wished you could tell everyone, the way Amy was."

Dory closed her eyes and sighed. "This is really awful for you, isn't it? You would have been mortified if I'd told Mary Ellen Wycliff, wouldn't you?"

"Lord, Dory, you might as well put it on the front page of the *Sun*. Mary Ellen knows everything and everyone, and tells everyone everything she knows. She sells more gossip in that boutique than she does dresses, and her classes just broaden her broadcasting base."

"You can't keep hiding from this, Scott. In a few more weeks, it'll be obvious that I'm pregnant. Are you going to hide me, then hide our baby? Am I supposed to stay away from Gainesville, or will I sneak up to your door so we can spend weekends isolated in your apartment? Will I have to sneak the baby in after it's born?"

Scott jerked up, pulling his arm from around her. Sitting on the edge of the bed, he combed his fingers through his hair and gave her a scowl filled with despair. "You're not being fair, damn it!"

"*You're* not being fair!" she snapped back, raising up on an elbow. "You can't go on pretending this hasn't happened. You can't relegate something as significant as a child to the status of an embarrassment."

"It *is* . . ." He swallowed the rest of the retort, buried his face in his hands and sighed miserably. His voice, when he spoke, was so soft it was barely audible. "It *is* embarrassing, Dory. In this day and age, a man is supposed to have more . . . to be—"

"That's lovely, Scott. That's just lovely! I'm thinking in terms of getting a house big enough for a baby, and adapting my entire life to include the total, awesome responsibility of raising a child. My father's telling me that if any attorney came into his courtroom unmarried and pregnant he'd hold her in contempt of court, and you're nursing your male ego! You knocked your old lady up. Yes, I can see how embarrassing that must be for you."

She picked up her pillow, plumped it fiercely with her fist and flopped on the bed like a grounded fish. Deliberately turning her back to him, she pulled the covers up to her chin and said, "I'm so terribly sorry this had to happen to sully your reputation."

Scott dropped back onto the bed. "Dory. . ."

"Don't touch me!" she seethed.

"Dory, please."

"Turn out the lights, Scott. The party's over."

Several minutes passed while Scott debated over what to do. For most of that time he stared at the unyielding set of Dory's shoulders. Finally, recognizing defeat when he stared it in the back, he got up, turned out the light, and crawled back in under the covers.

He waited until Dory was asleep before moving next to her and putting his arm around her. He was immensely relieved when, in her sleep, Dory snuggled up against him and sighed.

9

DORY WAS CATCHING UP on some neglected paperwork when her secretary beeped her and asked if she could speak to Dr. Sergei Karol.

Seconds later she said, "Hello, Dr. Sergei Karol. Do you know how impressive that sounds? No wonder you don't just say, 'This is Dory's brother—can she talk now?'"

"My office manager talked with your secretary," he explained. "And you won't be so cheeky when I tell you why I called."

"Okay, Big Bro, you got my attention. What's up?"

"I've got a peace offering. For—you know, my clumsy offer of the wrong kind of help."

"This had better be something big. Don't tell me—you've bought a Rolls, and you're handing down your Mercedes convertible to me."

"How about . . . Orlando?"

"Orlando. Florida?"

"How about a weekend at the Peabody Hotel? You can sit in the bar and watch the ducks waddle in and imagine how you're going to walk in a few months."

"Low blow, Sergei." *Why couldn't Scott joke with her this way?* "What's this all about, anyway?"

"I'm going to a seminar on new applications of laser surgery. I told you about it. Anyway, I screwed up and forgot to make room reservations, and all I could get was a suite, so I thought maybe you wanted to run away for the weekend with me. You could do some Christmas shopping at the outlet mall or go to Sea World. Can you clear Friday on your calendar?"

"Friday, as in day after tomorrow?"

"'Fraid so."

"You're on!"

"Great." He paused. "Dory?"

"Hmm?"

"We could make a jog by Gainesville on the way if Scott's free. I'll take the sleeper in the living room, and you two could take the—"

"That's not such a good idea."

Somehow the silence on Sergei's end of the line sounded sympathetic. Dory heard him inhale, then he said, "I'm sorry, Dory."

"Yeah," Dory said softly. "So is he, so am I. Everybody's sorry." She sighed defeatedly. "Sorry and seventy-five cents will get you a cup of coffee."

He arrived at her house Friday morning.

"Ready to hit the road?" he asked, picking up her garment bag.

"I've slathered my face with sunscreen, I'm wearing my scarf, and I have my stadium blanket in case the breeze gets chilly," she said. "Lead me to your convertible."

"So what's this?" Sergei asked, reaching out with his free hand to flip the long ears of the stuffed rabbit Dory had tucked under her arm, along with the blanket.

"His name's George," Dory said. "He belongs to the baby. We're kind of keeping each other company until spring."

"Anything you say," Sergei said with a you're-a-little-strange shrug.

The day was sunny and cool, a perfect Florida winter day ideal for zipping down the interstate in a Mercedes convertible. Dory, with the stuffed rabbit in her lap, pulled the stadium blanket over her chest and tucked it around her shoulders.

"Want to talk about what's-his-name?" Sergei asked, after they'd left the city for open highway.

"His ego is suffering," she said bitterly. "He finds a pregnant *significant other* rather embarrassing. He's afraid someone might think *he* slipped up."

"Give him some time, Dory."

"He's not going to adjust to it."

"I think you're wrong."

"Am I? He's had almost as much time as I have, and he still can't say *baby*. The very word sticks in his throat. If he wasn't trying so hard, I could be bitter or angry. But he *is* trying. He wants to care, but he can't find love inside himself for our baby. That scares the hell out of me."

"He doesn't have your well of experience to draw from, Dory. You know his family situation."

"What if he can't, ever? What if he never finds it?" Dory said. Swallowing the lump forming in her throat, she answered her own question. "I'm losing him, Sergei."

"Did you think it could last forever, the way things were?" Sergei asked. "Didn't you realize that eventually you'd want things a long-distance relationship couldn't supply?"

Dory closed her eyes, tilted her face toward the sun and sighed. "I guess I always thought that when I got ready for...tradition...he would, too. That we would make the decisions together."

"If Scott can't get used to the idea now, when a child is already a reality, chances are he never would."

Dory choked back a sob. "You don't need a scalpel to dig inside someone and find her greatest fear, do you, Dr. Karol? I can't stand to think that it's going to end this way, that Scott just isn't capable of making room for a child. I love him so much, and I know he loves me. It should follow that he would love our child."

"Logic and *shoulds* are for fairy tales and romance novels, Dory. Life isn't fair, and people aren't perfect. He may be trying—"

"He is. I know he is. And that makes it hurt all the more, because he's trying but he *can't*. I don't want to think of Scott being less than he could be, and he's a caring person. He'd be a wonderful father."

A cracking sound in her throat betrayed her struggle against tears. "I know he would, and I hate being *disappointed* in him. It would almost be easier to deal with another woman. At least I'd have the anger. If it ended in anger, that would be quick, like a guillotine. If we just gradually fall apart, it's going to be like our love is dying of some painful, lingering disease."

"Whatever happens, Dory, you'll get through it."

She looked at him, and gave him a wry smile. "Meaningless platitudes, bro? After you've been so brutally frank?"

He responded with a benign grin. "You'll have to get through it, little sis. Defeat isn't in the Karol family vocabulary."

"I wish I could delete a few other words from this Karol's vocabulary," Dory said. "Like misery, uncertainty and loneliness."

THE PEABODY DUCKS were making their morning march through the lobby by the time Dory made it downstairs on Saturday. She couldn't help grinning as the sleek mallards paraded in single file, their tail feathers swaying with each fall of their webbed feet. Such pomp and circumstance over a flock of ducks! The hotel guests, assembled and held at bay in the lobby because of the procession, reacted with titters of laughter, appreciative oohs and ahs, and self-conscious throat clearing by those too staid to admit they found redeeming social significance in such tomfoolery.

The lobby quickly cleared when the pageantry was over, and Dory took a shuttle to Sea World. She meandered through the park at an unhurried pace that matched a day gentle with sunshine and mild breezes. At first, awed by the size and majesty of killer whales passing sleekly through the water, amused by the antics of trained sea lions, enchanted by the cunning cuteness of an otter, she escaped the depression that had been stalking her since she'd left Gainesville the weekend before. She forgot for a while, as she studied the several species of penguins in the penguin encounter, how demoralizing it had been to wake up in the blissful haven of Scott's arms on Sunday morning only to remember the bitter words and unsolved problems of Saturday night—problems that still were unsolved, perhaps would remain insoluble.

She was surrounded by children. Babies slept in strollers, oblivious to the excitement around them.

Toddlers, enthralled by the barking and dancing of sea lions, regarded everything with bright, wide eyes. School-aged children ran to the wall of the tank in the Shamu stadium, hoping to be drenched by salt water splashed by a killer whale and squealing when the cold water rained over them. Preteens in motley fashions alternated between spurts of pseudosophistication and unruly giggles.

Some of the parents were harried and tired looking, some jolly, some serene, some smiling and indulgent, some cross and stern. Dory looked at them and wondered, as every pregnant woman wonders, what kind of mother she would be. And she wondered, the way no pregnant woman should have to, whether or not her child would know his father.

She stopped for ice cream in a waffle cone and remembered eating ice cream with Scott at Micanopy; she browsed in the souvenir shops and kept encountering tables filled with sets of mother and baby killer whales, plush likenesses of Baby Shamu, the first killer whale born in captivity, and his mother.

It was feeding time at the seal-feeding pavilion, and the walls of the sea lion and seal pools were lined with people tossing mullets or watching the sea animals cavort and cajole the tourists. A Sea World educator ruled over the mayhem from a small gazebo, cautioning parents not to sit children on the top of the ledge where they could fall or be pulled into the pool.

The sea lions, frisky and playful, rolled up their rear flippers, using them like feet so they could stand and beg. The seals, with their mottled brown and gray coats, and bushy whiskers and eyebrows, clowned less but were equally cunning. One bull rolled sideways in the water and waved with his fin, then barked angrily when he wasn't agile enough to catch a fish tossed by a little girl in a Mickey Mouse T-shirt. The younger seals won hearts with gentle pleas in their dark, round eyes.

Dory bought a tray of mullets and tossed one to the bull with the volatile disposition. Pleased with it, he rolled over in the water and waved a flipper at her. She would have sworn he was grinning. She threw him another fish, then aimed one at one of the babies in the middle of the pool. Grumpy let out a disgruntled roar. Dory laughed and tossed him the last of the fish.

The attendant was lecturing about sea lions and seals, detailing the similarities and differences between the two. "Both live in family units called rookeries. The males are called bulls, and the females are cows. The babies are called pups. A rookery usually consists of at least one bull, one or more cows and numerous pups."

Dory looked down at the seal pup she'd fed, into the pup's dark, pleading eyes, and whispered, "Lucky you, with a whole family around you." She toyed with the idea of buying another flat of fish, but decided against it. Instead she washed her hands at the nearby sink and walked to the front gate to wait for the shuttle back to the Peabody.

Sergei returned to the room earlier than anticipated and found her curled up on the sofa holding George the Rabbit to her bosom in a death grip. Her eyes were red-rimmed and swollen, and mascara smudges stained her cheeks. "Sergei!" she said. Then, realizing how much she'd made it sound like an accusation, she said evenly, "You're back early."

"I got buttonholed by a pediatrician concerned about a patient, and we got to talking about Orlando and decided to go over to Church Street Station for dinner and whatever." He paused and ran his fingers through his hair, as if concerned but not quite sure what to do about his distraught little sister. "You're invited along, of course."

"Does this . . . *pediatrician* know it'll be a threesome?"

Sergei struggled for a tactful reply, and Dory chuckled. "It's all right, Sergei. You don't have to mollycoddle me just because I'm a little down in the dumps."

"You can go," he said. "We'll probably run into dozens of people from the conference. Maybe a crowd would take your mind off—"

"Oh, no." Dory shook her head. "No, thank you. I don't think partying is the antidote to what ails me."

Sergei flopped down beside her. "You're obviously upset."

"It'll be okay, Sergei. Honest. All that fresh air today wore me out. I'll probably order something from room service and watch a movie."

"I hate leaving you here alone."

"Please, Sergei. I'd feel guilty if you canceled your date for me, and I wouldn't be any fun at Church Street Station in the mood I'm in."

"What set you off?"

Dory sighed. "Did you know that seals live in family units?"

"Somehow that little tidbit of knowledge seems to have eluded me."

"Bulls, cows and pups. Daddies, mommies and babies." A shrill sob rose from her throat. "Oh, Sergei, if seal pups have daddies, why can't my baby have one?"

Sergei put his arms around her, supplying a shoulder. "Your baby has a father, Dory. And if Scott doesn't come around, my niece or nephew is going to have one hell of an uncle. And I couldn't feel too sorry for any child with you for a mother."

Dory sniffed and raised her head to look at Sergei. "That's a sweet thing to say, Sergei. Do you really think I'll be a good mother?"

"You?" he said with a chuckle. "You're a natural. You've been nagging me ever since you learned to talk."

"Nagging?"

"Mother-type nagging, yes. You were always tying my shoelaces and straightening my collars and telling me to comb my hair. And remember when I was sweating getting into med school? You were the one assuring me I'd make it."

"But a baby, Sergei. I don't know anything about babies."

"What's to know? You'll feed it when it's hungry, hug it when it's scared and make sure it doesn't flush your favorite overcoat down the toilet."

"You're not exactly Dr. Spock, but you make it sound so . . . fundamental. So simple."

Sergei hugged her shoulders. "It will be, you'll see. You'll attack motherhood as wholeheartedly as you do everything else. You'll read books and go to parenthood preparation classes and compare notes with other mothers and drive your pediatrician crazy with middle-of-the-night phone calls the way all new mothers do. You'll survive, and the kid will thrive."

He gave her a mock-stern look. "Right?"

"Right," she said.

"Feeling better now?"

She nodded. "Crisis averted. Now go get gussied up for that pediatrician."

"Are you sure you don't want to go with us?"

"Now who's nagging? Would you quit babying me and get out of here?"

Later, after Sergei had left in a cloud of expensive men's cologne, Dory ordered boiled shrimp and spinach salad from room service and curled up on the sofa to watch the movie on cable. It was a feature she and Scott had seen at the theater months earlier, so it, as everything else seemed to do, reminded her of Scott and made her wonder what he was doing with his Saturday night.

She would have been shocked if she could have seen him at that moment.

10

SCOTT WAS UNDER ASSAULT. Ten-month-old Jessica Albertson, with a death grip on his knee, was regarding him with pleading eyes and reaching for the pretzel in his hand. "Cracker," she said, then repeated the entreaty several times to be sure he understood. "Cracker. Cracker. Cracker."

"What do I do?" Scott asked his best friend, business partner and father of the little beggar.

Mike rolled his eyes exasperatedly at Scott's helplessness and said simply, "What do you mean, what do you do? Give the kid a pretzel."

Scott took a pretzel from the bowl on the end table and cocked his head at Mike. "Are you sure about this? I thought babies ate strained spinach and disgusting stuff."

"She's been eating crackers and stuff for months. She sucks on them a while to soften them up."

"That's disgusting."

"You eat pretzels your way, and let Jessica eat pretzels her own way. Right, Jessica?" Mike said. Scott observed, with interest, the exaggerated smile Mike gave his daughter and the ga-ga tone of voice he used when he was talking to her. Mike, his partner, the no-frills, superanalytical accountant, was on the verge of talking baby talk.

Jessica answered her father's banter with a broad smile which she ficklely turned on Scott when he handed her the pretzel.

"Thank you," Mike prompted.

"Dank do," Jessica said, and then added, "Cracker."

"You're welcome," Scott said, feeling foolish. He turned to Mike. "How do you know when it's okay to give her crackers?"

"Well, in addition to the classes Susan took and the entire shelf full of baby reference books, the pediatrician gives her advice every time she takes Jessica in."

"Oh."

"It's all very regimented. I tell you, Scott, you wouldn't believe the baby business. Parents have got to be the most exploitable market outside of teenagers with rock tapes and stuff. If I wanted to make a million dollars, I'd invent something parents feel their child absolutely has to have, preferably something for the kid's health or education."

"Exploitable, huh?" Scott asked thoughtfully, watching Jessica gnaw at the pretzel.

"Like disposable diapers," Mike continued. "You think anybody washes diapers these days? Hell, no. They buy disposables. And buy them and buy them."

"Aren't they expensive?"

"Sure they are. But they're like cigarettes. People find the money for them, even if they can't afford them. There's a constant demand, and there's no recycling, like handing down clothes. Use 'em, then toss 'em, then buy more. When you think about it, it's fail proof. We ought to buy stock in Kimberly Clark. And Kodak. Did you ever see anybody who didn't have pictures of their kids? You go anywhere kids are, and there are parents with cameras. Click, click, click. The kid's born, click, click, click. The kid learns to sit up, click, click, click. The kid gets a tooth, click, click, click."

"What now?" Scott said. Holding the pretzel in her mouth, Jessica had her arm braced around his knee and her leg raised, trying to climb onto the sofa.

"I think she likes you," Mike said. "She probably wants in your lap."

Scott put his hands under Jessica's arms and lifted her up. She was heavier than he expected, dead weight like a sack of potatoes as he lifted, but she seemed much lighter as she settled into his lap.

"Scott," her father prompted. "Jessica, can you say, 'Scott'?"

"'Ott," Jessica mimicked, poking her soggy pretzel against Scott's lips.

"Isn't that sweet?" Mike said. "She's sharing with you."

Scott shifted his head from side to side dodging the pretzel. "Am I supposed to eat it? That wouldn't be healthy, would it? Germs..."

Laughing, Mike said, "Pretend to eat it." He demonstrated by taking a bite of air, working his jaw and saying, "Yum, yum."

Scott burst out laughing. "Yum, yum?" Jessica took advantage of his distraction and poked the pretzel between his lips. Scott pulled his head back and, feeling like a dim-wit, mimicked Mike, took an imaginary bite of the pretzel, then said, "Yum, yum."

Jessica giggled and prodded at his mouth again with the pretzel for an encore performance. They went through the routine five or six times before she tired of the game and turned around in his lap, settling her shoulders against his chest and watching the television as though she understood what was going on in the football game Scott and Mike were watching. Jessica's mother and a friend were giving each other permanents, so Jessica had been sent along with her daddy to Scott's apartment.

A few minutes later Mike said, "What do you know—she's fallen asleep."

Scott looked down at the child. Her head was tilted to one side and her lips were slightly parted. Her hair, the same shade of dark brown as her father's, curled in ringlets around her face. Scott was struck by how easily the child, so tiny and vulnerable, had trusted him.

"What's it like?" he asked Mike.

Mike was involved in the current play of the game. "Huh?"

Scott waited until the runner was tackled and the teams broke to rehuddle for the next down. "What's it like having a kid?"

"Sometimes it's a royal pain," Mike said. "I mean, it's constant. Unrelenting. Before we had Jessica, we used to leave double rations in the cat's dish and go off for the weekend on a moment's notice. Now if we go to a two-hour movie it's a major production—baby-sitter, instructions, worrying about how she's doing without us. And a weekend—geez, it's like loading up and going on the road with an entire circus. Clothes, diapers, food, portable crib, blankets, burp cloths, car seat, camera..."

"Is it—?"

"What?" Mike said, and reading Scott's mind, added, "Worth it?"

"I guess that's what I'm asking."

"Why the sudden curiosity?"

"I'm just trying to put it all together," Scott said. "We've known each other a long time, Mike. We raised some hell back in the undergrad days."

"I get a headache just remembering the hangover after the UF-Georgia game our senior year."

"We're still the same people, right? But I see you changing diapers and talking baby talk and I wonder how you can be the same person who used to sing twelve choruses to 'Roll Me Over in the Clover and Do it Again' at every victory party."

"We're the same people, Scott. We just grew up. At the height of the April tax crunch we break off at what—ten o'clock? Eleven? Yawning, moaning, groaning like old men. We used to put off major papers till the last minute then work straight through till morning. Now look at us—organized, sensible, wearing suits to work."

"We're the establishment types we used to point at and snicker," Scott said.

"And it doesn't feel so bad. Personally I don't mind driving a nice car instead of that old heap I couldn't keep running, and I sure as hell don't have any complaints about having Susan waiting for me after a hard day's work."

"And Jessica?" Scott said softly.

Mike's eyes drifted to the form of his sleeping daughter, and pride burned in them. "She's the icing on the cake, buddy. Sure, it's a hassle having a kid. But when I look at her, I see the future. And when she puts her arms around me and calls me Daddy, I feel . . ." He exhaled heavily. "I can't tell you how I feel. It's not something that you put in words. But it's like I grow, like she makes me bigger and better than I've ever been before."

Overwhelmed by the intensity of their discussion, they withdrew into the emotional safety of the football game. During the next station break, Mike took a quilt from the diaper bag Susan had packed and spread it on the floor. "She's out for the night," he told Scott. "I'll put her down before your arm falls off."

Gently he lifted his daughter from Scott's chest and eased her onto her stomach on the pallet, then covered her with a light blanket. She made a soft whimpering sound then snuggled against the quilt and quieted.

An odd, cool sensation, an emptiness filled the spot where the child had lain against Scott. To escape it, he got up and went to the refrigerator for beer.

"You and Dory finally getting a yen to settle down?" Mike asked, as Scott handed him a can.

Scott knew he'd been given the perfect opportunity to open up to Mike, but the lump of cowardice in his throat wouldn't let courageous words through. All he could do was voice his fear in the form of a question. "Don't you ever get tired of the constant accountability?"

"Sure, I get tired of accountability. I get tired of accountability to the mortgage company and the bank that financed my car, and the clients who expect perfection from us, and to the government and all the stupid forms we fill out, and the guys I play golf with who expect our foursome to make a respectable showing in charity tournaments."

"That wasn't what I asked, and you know it."

"Hell, yes, Scott, I know it. And yes, sometimes I get tired of having to call home if I'm going to be late, and having to be polite to Susan and cheerful to Jessica when I'm dog tired and all I want to do is collapse in my favorite chair and watch junk television or something. But I'm not going to get rid of my car because I get tired of paying a car note, and I'm not about to let go of what Susan and Jessica and I have just because sometimes I have to go beyond my own needs to accommodate theirs. Life is a trade-off, Scott. Everything has a price tag. I happen to think Susan and Jessica are worth the accountability. They're part of me, and I'm part of them, and I like it that way."

A sudden roar from the televised game drew their attention. One of the teams had intercepted a pass. "Aw-right!" Mike said as the runner reached the end zone and did a little dance.

"How can you stand it?" Scott said, oblivious to the game. "You keep books for twenty businesses simultaneously and could tell me to the penny what their account balance is on any given day, but you don't know how much money is in your own joint account."

Mike gave him an exasperated frown. "It's Dory, isn't it? What—is she putting the thumbscrews to you, getting tired of commuting?"

"How does an accountant stand having someone else inside his bank account?" Scott pressed, ignoring the questions that hit too close to home. "I've heard you call Susan a dozen times and say, 'Hey, have we got enough money for so and so?'"

Mike chortled. "If it bothered me, Susan and I would have separate accounts. It doesn't bother me. I'd trust Susan with my life, and I trust her implicitly with our money. She's got a level head when it comes to spending. She's never bounced a check."

"That's not the point," Scott said. "I'm talking about control. Doesn't it drive you crazy that you don't know how much is in your account at any given moment?"

Frowning, Mike turned in his chair to look at Scott full face. "What is this, an inquisition? An interview for *True Confessions*? You've got a problem with commitment, so you're not going to let me rest until I admit married life isn't perfect?"

Before Scott could form a reply, Mike went on, "Okay. It's *not* perfect. Sometimes Susan and I argue. Sometimes she even nags. You want to know what I miss about being single? I'll tell you. Remember when we used to get hungry in the middle of the night and hit the fast-food stands? Well, I don't hit the fast-food stands anymore."

He continued in a falsetto, comically mimicking his wife's voice, "Where are you going? McDonald's? That's ridiculous. What's that? You're dying for Filet-o-Fish?"

He paused for effect, warming to the performance. "You don't have to go out in the middle of the night for a fish sandwich. We've got a whole package of Mrs. Paul's filets in the freezer. Throw one in the microwave and stick it in a bun! Do you know how many drunks are on the road this time of night?"

Shaking his head, he resumed his normal voice and said, "Can you believe it? 'Throw it in the microwave and stick it in a bun!' No cheese, no special tartar sauce. The woman has no sense of tradition."

There was a silence. They looked at the television screen, but the players were milling around on the field while one of the coaches briefed a lineman during a time out. Mike said, "It was bound to happen, you know? Sooner or later."

Scott didn't reply. The teams lined up and put the ball into play. It wasn't until the next station break that Mike said, "You love her, don't you?"

Scott gave him an impatient frown. "You know I do."

"I'd rather have Susan than Filet-o-Fish sandwiches in the middle of the night. Any jerk in the U S of A can get a Filet-o-Fish for about a buck, but what Susan and I have between us can't be bought."

Noting the skeptical set of Scott's jaw, he said, "It's not perfect, but what is? All I know is that it feels good to be a part of her, and know that she's a part of me, and Jessica's a part of both of us. It's the way things were meant to be, otherwise there wouldn't be women and men and sex and children. What counts is that you find the right partner to begin with. Susan's right for me. What you have to decide is whether Dory's the right person for you."

He gave Scott a penetrating look. "I think you already know the answer to that one, buddy. What I can't figure out is why you risk not doing anything about it."

Scott stared stoically at the television screen. Mike shook his head in bewilderment and warned, "She's not going to wait forever, you know."

A muscle twitched in Scott's jaw. He knew. How well he knew!

The knowledge terrified him.

11

DORY ANSWERED the door with a sprig of mistletoe in her hand. She pulled Scott inside by the elbow and then held it over his head. Her smile was fetching, her eyes bright as she wished him Merry Christmas. She slid her arms around him, and covered his mouth with hers, intimately capturing the identical words as he spoke them.

They knew a moment of bliss, of seeming normality in the midst of turmoil. Scott feasted on sensations that seemed normal and right: Dory's lips, soft and open against his; her teeth and tongue, familiar in texture and taste; the full length of her body, lithe and warm against him. For as long as the kiss lasted, it was as though they'd never argued bitterly, as though Dory wasn't pregnant, as though they weren't both consumed by the fear that the pregnancy would tear them apart.

The kiss ended and they gradually moved apart. "Merry Christmas," Dory repeated breathlessly.

Scott thrust his fingers in her hair and cradled her head in his palm. His eyes burned over her face. "Are you my present?"

"Only one of several."

"I bet I'll like you best of all."

Dory guided his hand to her lips and kissed his palm, then smiled at him provocatively. "I plan to make sure you do."

Wrapping her hand around his, she led him toward the bedroom. He stopped in the entry to the hallway. "What's all this?" Although the living room had been in perfect order, a trail of cardboard boxes had turned the hallway into an obstacle course. "It looks like you're moving."

Dory grimaced, and said lamely, "I am."

Moving. Another change, major. Through the open bedroom door Scott could see the bed waiting for them with its covers folded back enticingly. The entire room was familiar, welcoming. But there were boxes stacked in the corner, waiting to be packed with her belongings. Dory was going to dismantle this familiar room, strip it and leave it empty. The shock of it hit him like a betrayal.

"I bought a house," she said. He turned to her and stared at her incredulously. "I know it seems kind of sudden," she went on, "but I've been thinking about buying a house. You know that. The tax advantage..."

She paused and sighed. "It just seemed like the right time to start looking. This is an adults only complex, so I'd have had to move sooner or later, and it'll be easier to move now, before..."

Her voice trailed off, but they both knew how she would have completed the sentence. Before she got awkward with pregnancy. Before she had a child to complicate the already complex process of moving. Scott felt the significance of it settle in his guts like a rock sinking to the bottom of a lake. The changes were inevitable. Changes in her body. Changes in their lives. Changes in their relationship.

"I found the perfect house. Oh, Scott, you're going to love it. It has a fireplace—you know how we've always talked about sitting in front of a fire. And I got a great deal. A VA loan with a no-qualification assumption. I had enough saved for half the equity, and Sergei's loaning me the rest so I don't have to hassle with any mortgage companies. It was just standing there empty, so I thought, 'Why not?' It'd be silly to pay rent here for another month when I could go ahead and move in."

She touched his face with her fingertips. "You'll help me move, won't you?"

Help her? Help her take apart the place they'd spent half their time together? Where they'd laughed together and made love? Help her destroy and abandon it?

"Scott?"

He forced a smile that was a lie. "Of course I'll help you."

Her body relaxed noticeably. "Oh, good. I'm hiring two of Adelina's friends from the college for half a day, so we should have plenty of muscle. Sergei's borrowing a pick-up truck if the weather's nice."

Sergei again. Scott liked Dory's brother, but it nettled him that Sergei was such a hero for her all of a sudden. He was usually too wrapped up in his medical practice to do much with his big brother role, but now . . .

A sigh of defeat slid silently through Scott's lips. Now that his sister was pregnant and alone, Sergei was stepping in to fill the role of supportive male presence. Scott knew he was being unfair, but he couldn't quell the resentment stabbing through him over Sergei's sudden involvement in Dory's life. Nor could he quell the self-loathing that followed hot on the heels of the resentment.

It was his own damned fault. He was the one who should be taking care of Dory, helping her make decisions, supporting her, encouraging her. Yet she hadn't discussed something as major as buying a house with him. She hadn't felt free to come to him. His indifference was driving her away. Yet he couldn't want what she wanted. He'd been trying. He couldn't be thrilled by this unwelcome, ill-timed intrusion in their lives, their love.

Boxes in the bedroom where they'd made love so often! *She was moving her life away from their past, just the way. . .*

Dory slid her fingers from his face into his hair, and cupped his ear in her palm. Standing on tiptoe, she pressed a small kiss on his cheek, then smiled up at him. "Weren't we on our way to something before we got sidetracked?"

Scott looked down at her face, the face he'd never tire of seeing. Love dwelled in the depths of her eyes, mingling with the sexual invitation, enhancing it. The fear that they might reach a point where he'd never see that look again overwhelmed him suddenly. He wrapped his arms around her, pulling her close to him, crushing her body against his, and kissed her deeply, urgently. Dancing would be a romantic interpretation of the way he half dragged her to the bedroom. He was incapable of loosening his hold on her. They stumbled along through the boxes as his hands roved over her body, slipping inside her blouse, savoring the feel of her flesh.

His kiss was relentless, probing, questing, demanding. Finally they tumbled onto the bed together, tearing at their clothes in frustration as the urgency of his need overwhelmed them both.

Cradling her hips in his hands, he thrust into her and moved in swift, deliberate strokes. She responded with fervor, locking her legs around him and pressing the heels of her feet into his buttocks. Her hands were filled with his shoulder muscles as she clung to him, as though letting go would mean sure and utter disaster. The kiss, the same wild, passionate mating of their mouths that had started in the hall, went on and on, unbroken, uninterrupted, becoming an imitative extension of their lovemaking.

The tension that had escalated so quickly culminated quickly, and Scott's mouth broke away from Dory's involuntarily to cry out with the intensity of it. He collapsed over her, breathing in huge gulps of air, relishing the warm solidity of her body pressed into his.

Reason crept back to him slowly. A strange whimper against his chest finally brought him back to awareness. "Dory? I didn't hurt you, did I?"

Another whimper. Panicking, he raised on one elbow. "Dory?"

She had been laughing softly, but, released from the weight of his body, she laughed fully now, rocking with mirth. This time he said her name with curious inquiry rather than concern. Her answer came strained through laughter. "I've heard of tearing into a p-pr-present, but you didn't even t-tr-try to save the r-ri-ribbons."

He looked at her, perplexed, not knowing how to handle her unexpected whimsical mood. Still laughing, she sat up and threw her arms around his neck and kissed him noisily on the cheek. "Merry Christmas." She kissed his other cheek. "Happy New Year." And his forehead. "Happy Valentine's." His left eyelid. "Happy Easter."

By Thanksgiving she had reached his mouth, and the kiss was genuine. When she drew away, Scott brushed a strand of hair from her cheek and said, "I didn't plan—"

A fresh gale of laughter interrupted him. "No one could have planned that."

"I didn't hurt you, did I?"

"Hurt me?" she asked, surprised by the notion. She lay back on the bed, looking up at him, and sighed. "I feel utterly desired."

"You're sure you're not . . . that I wasn't too rough?"

"You just don't know what it does for a girl's ego to be able to incite a man to mindless lust."

"You didn't come, did you? I didn't give you a chance."

Her smile was as smug as the Mona Lisa's. "You'll make up for it sooner or later."

She was still wearing her knit pullover and it had ridden down to cover her breasts. Scott slid his hand between the fabric and her skin, splaying his fingers over her ribs, then inching higher to tease the under-side of her left breast. He watched her face as his hand teased higher, roughing the tip of her breast with his palm. "How about sooner?"

She combed her fingers through his hair and guided his face to hers. "How about now?"

Instead of kissing her, he pulled away and nuzzled her shirt up with his nose to expose her breasts and buried his face in the valley between them. He flicked her skin with his tongue, then said, "I think you should have to wait awhile for laughing at me."

"I did not laugh at you!" she protested, then gasped pleasurably as he took the tip of one breast into his mouth and drew on it.

Her nipple hardened against his tongue. He abandoned it to kiss his way to the hollow of her throat and tease it with a flick of his tongue. "I think I should prove to you that my lust is not always mindless." He moved to her other breast, blew on the nipple and watched it swell in anticipation. "Or selfish," he added triumphantly.

It proved to be a long, thorough and eminently satisfying demonstration.

LATE THAT AFTERNOON, Dory tried to steal out of bed without disturbing Scott, but he grabbed her wrist just when she thought she'd managed to sit up without jiggling the bed. "Where are you sneaking off to?"

"The shower. I've got to start now if I'm going to get myself presentable in time for dinner."

He pushed her hair back away from her face. "You look presentable to me right now. Better than presentable."

Grinning, Dory said, "I'm talking about presentable, as in a public place. Only the fanciest places are open on Christmas Day. You don't mind going out, do you? I know I usually cook, but half the kitchen's packed and—"

"You know I don't mind. I brought a suit, just in case."

"Then I really have to get gussied up. All the women will be trying to lure you away from me."

Scott laughed, and Dory smiled. "They'll be looking at me, wondering how I got so lucky." *And I'll be wondering how much longer I'll be lucky enough to have you,* she thought desperately.

He noted the sudden sadness on her face. "What's wrong?"

Dory touched his cheek, then slid her arm around his neck and hugged him. "I need you so much."

"No more than I need you," he said. "If today didn't prove that, it's unprovable."

"Not just that way," she said. "Not just this."

Scott knew what she wanted to hear, but he couldn't say the words. The words would be easy. Feeling them, meaning them, fulfilling them would not. He couldn't say them without reservation, and it wouldn't be fair for him to say them less than wholeheartedly. He could tell her that he'd move to the suburbs and live with her in the house she'd bought, but the prospect struck fear in his heart—fear of the deterioration of the relationship that so far had been unflawed by the day-to-day stresses that generated resentment and bitterness and apathy.

Scott wanted to laugh with Dory, not discuss budgets. He wanted to make love to her because it was special between them, not take care of physical needs when they were both tense and tired. He wanted to talk about dreams and issues and whatever caught their fancy at the moment, not argue over toothpaste tubes and the countless picayune, inconsequential things people argued over when they lived together in close quarters. He wanted to come to her because he wanted her company, not when a clock struck a particular hour.

He wished he could find in himself the substance to be a husband, but he saw only the potential to be a lover, in every sense of the word. He loved Dory more than he'd ever expected to love a woman, perhaps even more than life itself. But he wanted a lover, not a wife. He wanted to be a lover, not a husband. He wanted someone to smile at him, not someone to nag him.

Dory gave his neck a brief goodbye kiss as she pulled away from him. She gave him a self-conscious grin and said, "Off to the showers."

The bed suddenly seemed big and empty, and Scott felt very alone in it. Partings now, even small ones, held an ominous undertone, a threat of impending permanence. Scott got up, pulled on his pants and wove his way through the maze of boxes in the hall to the kitchen for something to drink. Dory must have been packing in the kitchen when he arrived, because the cabinet doors were open, and the items from the top shelves had been emptied onto the countertop. The miscellany of serving bowls, cream and sugar bowls and salt and pepper shakers was accessible from the table, where a stack of blank newsprint could be used for wrapping.

Scott reached into the cabinet for a glass, but stopped as he caught sight of the wallpaper lining the back of the cabinet. It had taken him and Dory an entire weekend to line the cabinets. The cheerful print brought back memories of fighting the recalcitrant strips into place, meticulously butting the edges to match the prints, and of being sticky to their elbows with adhesive, and laughing as they playfully smeared each other's faces with the goo.

Dory had been so proud when they finished, so satisfied with it. And now she was leaving it behind.

Long ago, there'd been other wallpaper. Beautiful wallpaper with astronauts and spaceships on it. He'd picked it out with the solemnity that only a six-year-old child could garner, and supervised the papering of his bedroom walls with the mien of a man responsible for getting a job done right.

How he cherished that wallpaper! He lay on his bed on rainy afternoons and became one of the astronauts in the space suits with bubble helmets. In his mind he climbed into those spaceships and blasted off for voyages through the universe. He looked at that wallpaper and became a hero, a star voyager, just like the astronauts on television.

And then, one day, he came home from school to find his room empty and forlorn. He ran to his aunt, who was staying with him in the afternoons while his mother was in the hospital.

They'd taken his mother to the hospital in an ambulance with the lights flashing and siren screaming. His aunt arrived, and she and his stepfather had done a lot of whispering and shaking their heads, which scared Scott. Every time he asked about his mother, his aunt kissed his cheek and told him not to worry. But he'd worried silently, until finally they'd let him see his mother. He went to the hospital and she came to see him in the waiting room, riding in a wheelchair pushed by his stepfather. He hugged her tightly and told her he missed her and asked why she couldn't come home. She told him she had to stay at the hospital so she could have a healthy baby and assured him it wouldn't be too long. In just a few weeks he'd have a baby sister or brother.

"You'll be proud and happy to be a big brother, won't you?" she asked, but Scott didn't answer her. He wasn't at all sure he wanted to be a big brother, or that he'd be proud of a baby. Melinda had had two babies, and now Scott had to sleep on the couch when he visited his father, which wasn't as often as it had been before his stepbrothers had come along bim-bam, one right after the other. Before, he'd slept in a bed in the small bedroom of the apartment, but now that room was a nursery, and Melinda was afraid Scott would disturb the babies during the night.

"My room!" he cried, the day he found it dissembled. "What happened to my room? Where's my bed? And my books? And my toys?"

His aunt hugged him and assured him that his bed and belongings were just down the hall, in what had been his mother's sewing room. "You're grown up now, so you sleep all through the night. Your mother needs to have the baby in this room next to hers so she can hear it if it needs her."

"But my wallpaper!" Scott protested. "My astronauts."

"You're getting all grown up now, Scott. You don't need that kiddie wallpaper."

Scott choked back tears. He wanted to tell her that he did need that wallpaper, that it wasn't for kids, it was for space explorers, and he certainly wasn't too grown up to be a space explorer. Jerking away from his aunt, he ran down the hall and found his bed. His toys were there along with his books, all in boxes.

His aunt followed him. "Come on, Scott. We need to put the books back on the shelves. You can help me. I didn't know how you liked them, so I waited for you."

The books went back on the shelves, but the wall-paper wasn't moveable. Eventually it was replaced with ballerinas swirling in pink clouds which his mother said his stepsister would like. Scott felt cheated, brushed aside. His new stepsister was an interloper, a usurper. She had his room, nearest his mom, and she had wall-paper, while he had involuntarily been made to give up his astronauts and spaceships for pale blue paint. He wasn't a space explorer anymore. He was grounded, stranded in his mother's old sewing room without a single spaceship or hope of rescue.

"CHEESE," Dory said and moved aside so Scott could sprinkle a handful of grated Swiss into the fondue pot. She stirred the fondue to melt the newly added cheese.

After all the confusion of the moving, they had de-cided to welcome the New Year with a quiet party for two instead of going out.

Once the cheese was melted, Dory poured in a cup of white wine and transferred the pot from the stove to the fondue stand which she'd set up on the coffee table in front of the fireplace. She and Scott sat cross-legged on big floor pillows they'd shopped for earlier in the day and dunked chunks of bread, ham and salami into it.

Alternately ignoring and heeding advice from Dory, Scott had laid the fire with a stack of wood they'd bought at the supermarket along with the groceries for the fondue and gourmet ice cream for dessert. The weather was mild, hardly conducive to a fire, but they managed to keep the room comfortable by opening the windows a few inches.

The flames in the fireplace and the candle warming the fondue provided the only light as they supped on the fondue, mocking each other's efforts to get cheese on the bread without losing it in the bog, and then to get the coated chunks to their mouths without dripping strings of molten cheese on their clothes. When the fondue was gone they ate the ice cream, then, complaining that they'd eaten too much, they put their pillows side by side and lay down in the semi-darkness.

Since Scott's arrival they'd been too busy packing and unpacking for this lazy type of communion. Grateful for the quiet moment, Dory reached for Scott's hand, threaded her fingers through his and sighed. "Do you like the house?"

"I've told you I do."

"Once I get the study set up as an office, I'm going to get a computer and hook it up by phone modem to my computer at the office so I can work at home on the days I don't have consultations or court appearances."

"You should enjoy that."

"I'll still need full-time child care, even when I'm here, but I'll be close enough to visit with the baby throughout the day."

Scott didn't comment. Dory felt a lump forming in her throat, the same lump that always formed in response to his obvious reticence about the baby. Moving had tired her, and her tolerance to frustration was low. She felt like lashing out at him, kicking and screaming, until he stopped avoiding the issue, but she hadn't the energy to confront him or the will to ruin the holiday, so she said nothing.

Eventually the silence grew less charged with the unspoken issue between them. The knot in Dory's throat dissolved. Scott squeezed her hand gently and whispered, "This is nice. I'm glad we decided to stay in."

"Me, too," Dory whispered back.

They lay there listening to the crackling of the fire and watching shadows dance on the cathedral ceiling for a long time. Then, in the midst of serenity, Dory felt a slight squiggle in her womb. She held her breath, remained perfectly still, wondering if it could be the baby. She felt it again, another tiny squiggle, more definite this time because she was waiting for it, and gasped at the unexpected wave of emotion that surged through her at the faint evidence of life.

"Dory?" Scott said.

She turned her face toward his and smiled. "I felt the baby move." She laughed delightedly. "I felt it move!" She guided his hand to her abdomen, and pressed his palm over her womb. "Maybe, if it moves again, you can feel it."

But the baby moved, and Scott couldn't feel it. "Are you sure?" Dory asked, disappointed. "Just a tiny little wiggle?"

Scott shook his head helplessly.

"I guess it's not big enough yet, not strong enough for you to feel it from the outside." Scott started to move his hand, but she held it there, over her womb. "It'll feel your warmth, your presence."

"Do you really think so?" Scott asked.

"Probably not," said Dory. "It's surrounded by fluid. Very well protected. But I like your hand there anyway. It makes me feel—" her voice thinned to a stringy whisper "—as though you care."

"I do care, Dory," he said softly. "About you, and about the baby."

"I'm glad," she said, pressing her eyes closed to block tears. She shifted her head from the pillow to the crook of his shoulder and listened to the reassuring beat of his heart. "I'm so very glad."

"I want to know our baby. I want our baby to know me, to know I'm his father."

"He will," Dory said, snuggling closer to Scott. "He will."

When the New Year came, she was asleep there next to him. Scott hadn't the heart to wake her, so he kissed her forehead and whispered, "Happy New Year," so softly that she didn't stir. He slept, too, for a while, but woke up in a couple of hours stiff from the hardness of the floor. He roused Dory just enough for her to cooperate by getting to her feet, then guided her, still half-asleep, to the welcome softness of the bed.

THE NEXT MORNING they laughed about their wild New Year's Eve, and initiated the New Year by making love. Then, in the afterglow of their lovemaking, Dory said, "I've been thinking, Scott."

Scott's scalp prickled. "About what?" he asked, not really wanting to know. Her voice, the sober expression on her face told him whatever she was bringing up was serious and possibly unpleasant.

"If you're serious about wanting to know the baby—"

"I'm not going to ignore our child, Dory."

"I think . . ." She paused, exhaled a strained sigh and began again. "If you were just an acquaintance . . . I mean if you were a casual friend, or a client, and I wasn't so involved in this . . . situation . . ."

Scott sucked in a deep breath as he waited for her to go on. "I would advise you to see an attorney."

It wasn't what he was expecting. He let out a nervous laugh. "An attorney?"

"To talk about paternal rights."

Chafed, Scott said, "You're my attorney."

"But it wouldn't be ethical for me to give you advice. I'm too involved in the situation."

"What are you talking about, Dory? A contract, something in writing?"

Scott hurt when he looked at the anguish in her eyes as she nodded. "We've never needed anything in writing between us," he said. "We've always talked about trust, and how hypocritical contracts are between people who are supposed to trust each other."

"It's always been just us," she said. "There's someone else involved now, Scott. You can't go on pretending there isn't. Last night I felt our child move inside me. Soon my pregnancy will be obvious, and ultimately, there's going to be a baby. We have to think about the child."

"A contract seems so . . . cold. I just don't like it."

"Liking is irrelevant at this point, Scott. We're dealing in hard facts in a complex situation. Please, see an attorney. Have him draw up a contract and send it to me. I'll read over it and we can negotiate any areas of disagreement."

"Negotiate areas of disagreement? Listen to yourself, Dory. You sound like you're in a courtroom. This is me you're talking to. We've never needed anything in writing between us."

"We've never had a baby before."

A prolonged silence stretched between them. Dory reached out for him, needing to touch him, sensing his need for reassurance. She rested her fingers on his cheek lightly. "Things could change, Scott. Things we can't control." His jaw tensed under her fingertips. "If something happened to me, you'd want to have some say in what happened to our child, who would get custody. A contract would assure you that right."

He remained stubbornly quiet.

"I could get killed in traffic," she persisted. "Or murdered, or struck by lightning."

"Don't say that!"

Dory pushed up on one elbow. "We have to be realistic. We've produced a child. We have to be prepared for any eventuality. Do you think that because Scott Rowland loves me, I couldn't get hit by a concrete mixer? Or some lunatic couldn't come charging into the courtroom and shoot everyone in sight? I would feel better knowing that if it happened, there would be someone watching out for our child."

Scott pulled her into his arms and hugged her tightly against him. "I couldn't bear it if something happened to you."

"Yes, you would," Dory said. "You'd hate it, and you'd hurt, but you'd bear it and eventually go on. I would just feel better if I knew you had the legal means to make sure our child was cared for the way we'd want it cared for."

"I'll do it, then. For your peace of mind."

"Good," Dory said. "Thank you."

Scott kissed her forehead and her eyelids. "Just don't let anything happen to you, huh?"

"Why do you think I bought black-eyed peas for lunch today?" she asked lightly, referring to the Southern custom of the peas bringing good luck throughout the coming year if eaten on New Year's Day.

"For the money, of course," Scott said wryly. A variant version of the superstition was that every pea eaten on New Year's Day meant a dollar acquired in the year ahead.

"That's why I bought two cans!" Dory countered. "Might as well get all the bases covered."

12

"SERGEI!"

"I came to claim the steak dinner you promised for my help in getting you moved."

"I . . . Sergei, I'm not prepared."

"I had a feeling you'd say that. That's why I stopped at Publix on the way. Now that I know you're home, I'll get the groceries."

He'd thought of everything: steak, potatoes, sour cream, fresh green beans, lettuce, tomatoes, cucumbers, even charcoal for the grill. He lit the coals, while Dory seasoned the steaks, then they sat down to talk while the coals burned down to glowing embers for cooking.

Sergei stretched his long legs out in front of him and spread both arms on the back of the sofa, leaned his head back and exhaled heavily. "I'll tend the steaks, but other than that, I intend to be pampered, little sis."

"Rough day?"

"Seven surgeries, back to back."

"Poor baby," Dory said, exaggerating her sympathy.

"Speaking of babies, how is my future niece or nephew faring?"

"The little scamp's destined to be a soccer star."

"Moving around already?"

"Kicking up a storm," Dory said exuberantly. "I could hardly feel it at first—you know, you're not quite sure whether it's the baby moving or indigestion. Well, now I can tell."

"And you?"

"I seem to stay tired. My iron was low."

"Sounds like you're typically pregnant. Your doctor prescribed supplements?"

"Three horse pills a day."

Sergei laughed. "Good girl. So how did the Lamaze class go?"

"It was okay."

"Don't bowl me over with your enthusiasm," Sergei said.

"Sorry," Dory said with a small shrug. "I just felt a little conspicuous." She let out a titter of nervous laughter. "I guess I'd better get used to it, huh? I'll be showing soon, and there's no ring on the third finger of my left hand, so I'll be in for a lot of curious looks and raised eyebrows."

She had been wringing her hands. She looked down at them, discovered what she was doing and stopped. "I didn't think it would be this embarrassing. We're approaching the turn of the twenty-first century, not the twentieth. Single women who aren't even involved in caring relationships decide to have babies, and have them. Suddenly, Bap! I'm pregnant, and I'm happy about it. No apologies or defensiveness." She sighed softly. "I think mother and father's attitude have made me self-conscious. I really do care what they think, even if they infuriate me."

"I'm sorry I can't be your Lamaze partner, Dory. It's just my crazy schedule."

"You've got a demanding career, Sergei. You don't even have time for a personal social life. You can't be expected to take on the role of surrogate father to your pregnant sister's child."

"I should have at least gone with you the first time. Given you a little moral support."

"Everyone would have assumed you were my husband, then we'd have had to explain that you were my brother, and they'd have been just as curious."

Sergei still looked as though he felt guilty. She said, "Your concern means a lot to me, Sergei, but you didn't get me into this, and you can't protect me from people with prehistoric ideas. Hey, if it'll make you feel any better, I may have a partner by the next class session."

"Oh?"

"My instructor knows a widow who's a registered nurse. She worked in obstetrics for years, but now she's semiretired. She likes to work on special assignment from time to time, so my instructor is going to call her and see if she'd agree to go through the classes with me and coach me during labor."

"That sounds like the ideal solution to your problem."

"A *workable* solution," Dory said.

"But not a perfect one?"

"Nothing's ever perfect."

"Scott would be."

Dory gave him a little smile. "I wish you'd quit reading my mind. It's very disconcerting having one's mind read."

"I'm no mind reader." He grinned mischievously. "Just brilliantly perceptive. You went to class with a dozen pregnant women, and all of them had a husband with them except you."

"One of them brought her mother—her husband's a cop. He works nights."

"All right. Ten of them had husbands, one had a mother, and you didn't have anybody. Add that to the way I know you feel about Scott and this baby, and it's not difficult to deduce that you'd want Scott with you."

"I keep on wanting what I can't have. Does that make me a masochist, or just plain stupid?"

"It makes you perfectly normal," Sergei assured her. "You're in love, and you're having a baby. There's nothing abnormal about wanting the man you're in love with here with you, participating in all the excitement."

"I thought I was making such progress in accepting everything. Especially when I bought the house. When I was trying to make the final decision, I realized the reason I hadn't bought a house before was that way back in my subconscious I was waiting until Scott and I could buy a house together."

She shook her head slowly. "You should have been a psychiatrist, Sergei. The human mind is so amazing. All along Scott and I agreed that what we had was so great we didn't need any more. We talked about the beauty of it, the perfection of it. No petty demands, no petty grievances. Just a blissful sharing of our lives when we could get together. I didn't even know I was waiting for more."

She turned to look at him full face, and her expression was grave. "I was marking time, waiting for the very things we were scoffing at. Yet even though buying a house made so much sense, and renting an apartment made so little sense, I never even took the first step because I was waiting, waiting for the time when Scott and I went together to pick out a home. Not a tax advantage, or a wise investment. A home for the two of us and a family."

"Did you tell Scott all this?"

"I can't blackmail him into wanting it. I couldn't live with him wondering if he'd rather be in Gainesville, unencumbered."

"That's a hell of a word, Dory. Unencumbered. You're encumbered up to your armpits. Is it fair for him to be unencumbered? You didn't make this baby all by yourself."

"I could have taken the pill."

"Scott could have done without."

Dory scowled at him. "Why do men always have to be so crude."

"We just have a more . . . fundamental outlook than women," Sergei said. "The point is, both of you took the chances, and only one of you is having to live with the consequences. That's not fair, no matter how you look at it."

"Life's not fair," she said. "Now, I want to change the subject. What do you think of the house?"

"You've done wonders with it in just over a week. I suppose What's-his-name helped hang the pictures."

"Yes, he did. And he's going to line the cabinets for me like he did at the apartment, as soon as I pick out the pattern."

"Saint Scott."

"Please don't, Sergei. I could pressure him for anything I wanted and get it, but I don't want anything I have to pressure for."

"That's very noble, Dory, but it's very impractical. I hope you're at least hitting him up for child support."

"The subject has been broached, in a roundabout way."

Sergei rolled his eyes. "How roundabout? Dory, don't be dumb about this in the name of pride and independence."

Dory sat up stiffly. "Scott's very generous by nature. He said he'd like to help financially."

"I hope you didn't make a grand gesture and tell him you didn't need his help."

"He's seeing an attorney about a paternal rights contract." She rose abruptly and turned toward the kitchen. "I'm going to snap the beans and get them on. Don't you think you'd better check the coals? You're beginning to sound a lot like dear old Dad."

Sergei followed her into the kitchen and put his hand on her shoulder. "I'm in your corner, Dory. I didn't mean to upset you. I just don't want to see your—the way you feel about Scott—interfere with your common sense."

"The way I feel about Scott has done nothing but enrich my life," Dory replied somberly. "This baby—" She put her hand over her womb, then smiled at Sergei. "It's moving again." She paused, devoting full attention to the fluttering movements inside her. She looked squarely at Sergei. "I love this baby so much. Scott will, too. Wait and see."

Her expression changed and lighted with desperation. "Oh, Sergei, you don't think I did it on purpose, do you? That I just conveniently ignored the fact that water would wash away the cream?"

"Has Scott accused you of that?"

"No. It's just...it seems such a careless thing to have done."

He put both his hands on the balls of her shoulders. "If you were...*careless*, it was a subconscious decision, not a conscious one."

"The subconscious? You mean the same part of my brain that was waiting on Scott to buy a house?"

"I'm not saying it was a voluntary decision at all, but if it was...Dory, sometimes our subconscious knows what we really want better than our conscious. Our conscious gets all fouled up with logic and what we think we should want."

"You think I wanted a baby and wouldn't face it?"

"I've never seen a woman—any woman—as enchanted by pregnancy as you are. When I suggested—" his face colored "—what I suggested, you were livid. Fierce. Like a mother tiger protecting your young. If you were at all ambivalent about wanting a child now, I'd say you probably just slipped up, but—"

"So you think I might have—"

"I don't see that it matters one way or the other. The fact is that you're going to have a baby, and you're perfectly happy being barefoot and pregnant."

Together they looked down at Dory's toes peeping out from under the hem of her kaftan. Dory was the first to laugh, giggle really, then Sergei joined in.

KATE O'BANYAN STERLING, registered nurse, was as imposing as her name. She was affable, but crisply aloof. Her voice was pleasant, but held a note of unbreachable authority. She had agreed to meet Dory prior to the childbirth preparatory class and, because of the timing, the two women had met at a restaurant for dinner.

It was Kate who'd suggested that, because they would be working together so intimately as a team, they should start out immediately on a first-name basis. She was younger than Dory had expected. Her retirement, she explained, was ten years premature because she had left her hospital job to nurse her husband during the last months of his terminal illness. Since his death, she'd worked only part-time, filling in when the nursing shortage grew acute during flu epidemics or peak vacation seasons.

"I've attended hundreds of births, although never as a coach," she told Dory, after giving a brief summary of her professional training. She liked, she had stated in the beginning, to take care of business up front.

She went on in her crisp, businesslike drone. "This arrangement would be unconventional, but I think it would work. However, I'm not sure how your insurance company will view it. They might not consider childbirth preparatory classes a legitimate justification for hiring a private nurse."

Nonplussed by Kate's directness, Dory gazed at her blankly.

"Do you understand what I'm saying?" Kate asked. "They may not reimburse you for my fees."

"I . . . uh, to tell you the truth, I hadn't even considered filing a claim. I suppose it would make sense to try, and if they honored it, fine. If not . . . well, I guess I'd have to take care of it personally."

"This is the first time I've done anything like this, but I thought half my normal daily fee for each class and a full day for the actual labor, unless it runs over eight hours, at which point we prorate it hourly." She paused, and when Dory didn't say anything added, "The classes are only two hours each, but there's commuting time, and disruption of my personal schedule, so the half day..."

"Oh, it sounds very fair," Dory said. "Do you want payment in advance?"

"I'll invoice you monthly during the classes," Kate said. "And then after the delivery. The invoices might give some legitimacy to the insurance claim."

Dory nodded. "About the labor..."

Kate raised her eyebrows interestedly. "Yes?"

"My brother is a physician, and he plans to scrub for the delivery. He won't interfere with what we're doing or what my doctor does. I just thought you might want to know he plans to be there."

"Karol," Kate mused. "Dr. Sergei Karol?"

"Yes. He's my brother. Do you know him?"

"I've heard his name at the hospital. A surgeon. Excellent reputation. I'll look forward to meeting him."

By the end of their first class together, Dory was convinced their partnership was going to work. She already felt less self-conscious now that she had a partner, and she had a feeling that in an emergency, Kate would be a good person to have on her side, skilled, tenacious and efficient. Kate even made a number of wry comments during class that revealed an unexpected sense of humor.

All the way home Dory puzzled over her lack of relief at having found a workable solution to a vexing problem. She liked Kate, felt comfortable with her and **had** confidence in her skills as a nurse. But something about Kate O'Banyan Sterling nettled her, something

Dory couldn't quite put her finger on. She found the riddle unsettling until, finally, she was able to isolate what it was about Kate that irritated her. In the middle of a long, sleepless night, Dory finally realized Kate's fatal flaw: she wasn't Scott.

Dory didn't want a nurse, she wanted a husband. She tossed and turned for what remained of the night, then dragged herself from the bed and dressed for work. She was down to two dresses that didn't grow unbearably uncomfortable by the end of the day, and one of them had never been a favorite. She felt not only tired, but frumpy, since her only comfortable work shoes did not coordinate with the dress. Forced to choose between style and comfort, she chose comfort, deciding she could stay reasonably hidden behind her desk for the three consultations she had scheduled for that day.

As the day progressed, she was overwhelmed by the state of things in general—her unrelenting fatigue, exacerbated by her sleepless night; the frumpishness imposed on her by a dwindling wardrobe of clothes that fit; having a nurse instead of a husband for a partner in her childbirth preparation classes. She was falling behind at work, and she desperately needed to shop for some office clothes. She was supposed to leave for Gainesville after work, but the hundred and fifty miles between her apartment and Scott's loomed more like a hundred and fifty light-years in her mind.

At precisely three o'clock, after one consultation had run over and another client was seated in the outer office waiting to see her, Dory realized she could not go to Gainesville. She simply could not go. She felt like crying in frustration, but squared her shoulders instead and dialed the back line at Scott's office.

Scott offered to come to Tallahassee.

"I don't think that would be a good idea," she said wearily.

"I don't mind driving, if you're not feeling well. I want to see you."

"No, Scott. Please. I wouldn't be good company, and I've got ten thousand little errands to run."

"Are you sure?"

"Yes."

"Maybe next weekend."

"Yes. Next weekend." She hung up the telephone, groaned in sheer frustration, then buzzed her secretary over the intercom and instructed her to send in the client who was waiting to see her.

Scott hung on to the receiver long after the line went dead, battling fury and frustration. This was the second time Dory had canceled a trip to Gainesville. Those cancellations, his impromptu Thanksgiving jaunt to Tallahassee and the holidays had wreaked havoc on their long-established pattern of alternate weekend visitations. Nothing was the same anymore, and he didn't know how to stop the changes or reestablish the old patterns that had worked so well for them.

He could feel the emotional distance between them growing into an unbreachable gap, far more handicapping to their relationship than the physical distance between Gainesville and Tallahassee ever had been. First a house, now some flimsy excuse for not coming to Gainesville. Tired! She might be tired, but he'd heard something else in her voice. Something was wrong, something she wasn't letting him in on.

His fist hit the top of his desk with a force that rattled the pens in his drawers and vibrated the computer monitor. Damn it! He wasn't going to let it happen. Dory wasn't going to shut him away from her. She could buy houses without telling him and cancel weekends claiming she was tired, but she wasn't going to ease him out of her life.

13

SOMETHING NUDGED DORY, raising her from deep sleep to a cozy, replete state of half sleep. She wiggled under the covers, searching again for that state of absolute oblivion, and hit something warm and wonderful. Instinctively she cuddled against it, drawing reassurance from that warmth. "Scott?" she murmured.

"Yes, Dory. It's me."

"Good," she mumbled. "I'll sleep better now."

"Go back to sleep."

With a sigh, she did as instructed, with her body spooned against his. His arm was under her neck, supporting her with its hard strength.

In the morning she decided it had been a dream, until she hugged Scott's pillow and smelled his after-shave there. Coming more fully awake, she was aware of odd scraping noises in the living room. "Scott?" she called.

A few seconds later he appeared at the bedroom door, fully dressed, screwdriver in his hand. "Good morning," he said, smiling.

"Good morning," she replied automatically, then added, "Scott?"

"You were expecting the meter reader maybe?"

"I wasn't expecting anyone," she said. "When...? Why...? I thought I'd dreamed you."

"It's me, in the flesh. Want to pinch me to make sure?"

"No. But—"

"I got here just before midnight. The lights were all out, and I didn't want to disturb you, so I changed in the front bathroom."

"But why are you here? I thought we agreed—"

"We didn't agree, Dory. You said you wouldn't be fit company, and I fumed till around nine o'clock, and then decided I'd still rather be with you tired than sulking around by myself all weekend, so I threw some clothes in the car and here I am."

Dory was so glad to see him that she was treacherously close to tears. "Oh, Scott."

He sat down on the edge of the bed. "Before you start lecturing, let me say that I'm not going to demand anything from you for this entire weekend. In fact, I'm going to wait on you hand and foot, unless you really don't want me here, in which case you can tell me right now and I'll leave."

Dory lunged for him, throwing her arms around his neck. "Oh, Scott, I've never been so happy to see anyone in my whole life."

Scott laughed, his delighted belly laugh that made Dory feel good all over just to hear. "That's more like it." He gave her a brief kiss on the cheek and then slid his hands down to her wrists and took her arms from around him. He kissed each of her palms, then guided her hands into his lap. "Now why don't you tell me why you really didn't want to come to Gainesville."

"I told you; I was tired."

"That much was obvious, considering that I broke into your house and got in your bed last night and you didn't even stir until I shook you."

"You broke in?"

"I don't have a key yet—the key shop was out of blanks, remember?"

"Then how . . . ?"

"All your lights were out, and I hated to wake you, so I decided to try to pick your lock. It was a piece of cake, lady. I could have been a crazed ax murderer and you wouldn't have known I was here."

Dory leaned forward and nuzzled her cheek against his chest like a cat and chuckled sensuously. "I'd have known when you got in bed."

"That might have been a little late, don't you think?"

"I was bushed," she said defensively. "And I listened to my self-hypnosis relaxation tape when I went to bed. That always zonks me out."

"I'm delighted you got some rest, but now I have to make sure I do. I've already bought dead bolts, and I'll have them installed within the hour."

"You what? What time is it?"

"Ten. The hardware store opens at eight-thirty. I also stopped at the supermarket for fresh-squeezed orange juice and apple crumb muffins."

Voice cracking, Dory reached up to hug him and said, "You're going to make me cry, and you know how I hate to cry."

"I'm only trying to pamper you."

"I know, but you're so sweet, and it's so good having you here when I wasn't expecting . . ."

"Why don't you take a shower while I finish installing the locks, then we can have breakfast, and you can tell me all about those nasty errands we're going to run."

A few minutes later Dory stepped out of the shower and heard Scott whistling as he worked in the living room. An odd sense of contentment filled her. She'd never loved Scott more than at this moment. This was the second time he'd shown up unexpectedly just when she needed him. And now he was installing locks to keep her safe. He'd been so righteous, so protective when telling her about having bought them, so assertive about getting them installed—as though expecting her to protest—that she wasn't about to tell him dead bolt locks were on her list of things to take care of.

There was a loud thunk, followed by a curse. A smile formed on Dory's lips. It was so homey having him here, taking care of her. Just like a husband.

Just like a husband? She rolled her eyes at her reflection in the mirror. This wasn't the first time Scott had puttered around doing handyman-type work at her place. Why was she suddenly thinking in terms of a husband? Was it the fact that a house just seemed homier than an apartment, or was it hormones? She attacked her wet hair with the towel and frowned. Hormones, no doubt. Or her subconscious. Whatever it was, she refused to dwell on it. Scott was here; she was going to enjoy it.

He was waiting at the table by the time she'd dried her hair and dressed in the only pair of pants she could still button and a shirt meant to be baggy. Scott poured the orange juice and grabbed a muffin from the bakery box. "So what are these terrible, dark errands we're going to see to today?"

Dory swallowed her first bite of muffin and took a sip of juice. "These are delicious."

"Don't hedge, Dory. Whatever it is, we're in it together. I'll even clean gutters or do windows."

His earnestness was too appealing; Dory couldn't hold back a smile. And a slight blush. "It sounds so feeble."

"Whatever it is—"

"I've got to go shopping!" she confessed.

It was Scott's turn to laugh. "For what?"

"Everything!" Dory said. "Oh, Scott, I don't have any clothes that fit. I'm not quite ready for maternity clothes, but everything's so uncomfortable, except that horrible dress I bought on sale that time, the green one with the Peter Pan collar. And I can't wear heels, and the only dressy flats I have are my brown pumps, and I had to wear them with that awful green dress and hope my clients couldn't see behind the desk."

"All right," Scott said. "Work clothes and flat shoes."

"And I've got to have loose pants for my classes."

"Classes?"

"My natural childbirth preparatory classes. I also need a pillow, so I don't have to keep taking one off the bed. Kate says if I don't want to get maternity pants yet, I could try fleece sports pants with a tie waist, but fleece is awfully warm, so I probably ought to go ahead and get at least one pair of maternity pants."

"Who's Kate?"

"Kate? She's a nurse. She's going to be my partner in the classes, and coach me during labor."

"Your coach? I thought—"

"She's very competent," Dory said quickly, before he could complete the thought. "She's worked in obstetrics for years, and she's considering studying to become a licensed midwife."

"What else?"

"Isn't that enough?" Dory asked. "The only way she could be more qualified is to have a medical license."

"I was talking about our shopping spree. Are clothes all we have to shop for?"

"All?" Dory repeated incredulously. "Scott—dresses, shoes, pants. It's everything. It's monumental. It's—"

"Since when is shopping a chore for you?"

"Since I have to start all over. Scott, I don't know how to shop for clothes that don't touch me anywhere. I'll probably look like a blimp in anything, just like I do in that stupid green dress."

"Just don't get anything with a Peter Pan collar," Scott said, just before succumbing to laughter.

"What's so funny?" Dory said, bristling in the face of his amusement. "It's not funny," she protested, and when that did nothing to quell his high-spiritedness, insisted, "It's not! Scott, I'm pudgy! And I don't appreciate your laughing at me."

"Dory, listen to yourself. You're not pudgy; you're pregnant. And you sound like a pregnant lady."

She was absolutely quiet a moment, and then she laughed. "I sound like a pregnant lady." As quickly as her laughter had flared, it subsided, and a serious expression claimed her face.

"Dory?" Scott asked, concerned.

She reached across the table to touch his face. "I just realized how glad I am that you're here." *And how much I love you.*

He captured her hand and kissed it. "If you keep looking at me like that, we're never going to make the mall."

"Would that be so awful?"

"It wouldn't be honorable," Scott said. "I came to help you deal with all your pressing problems, not interfere with them. I promised I wouldn't demand anything from you this weekend and I meant it."

"Not even?" she asked suggestively, giving him an unmistakable come-hither look.

"Especially not that!" he said. "I took a vow of celibacy for the weekend."

"You did not."

"I did. I don't take advantage of tired, pregnant ladies. Now eat your muffin like a good little mother. We've got a lot of shopping to do."

After trying three shoe stores, Dory finally found a comfortable pair of leather-and-snakeskin pumps in a neutral taupe-and-gray blend. There was a maternity shop near the shoe store, and she found a pair of khaki pants and a chic tailored dress-and-jacket suit on sale. Feeling triumphant, she and Scott stopped for a late, lingering lunch in an isolated corner of Ruby Tuesday's.

They went through the career department of several stores and were growing discouraged before finding a solicitous saleswoman. Desperate, Dory explained her special needs.

"So you want something loose,‚ but that projects a professional image," the woman summarized.

"But no Peter Pan collars," Scott interjected, and Dory gave him a friendly elbow in the ribs. She was past humor in their quest.

"I think I know just the thing," the woman said, and led them to an entire rack of coordinates. Dory found an unsculptured gray jacket with wide lapels edged in crisp black braid, and two coordinating sheath dresses, one ice gray and the other a deep charcoal which, un-belted, were comfortable, but suggested the idea of a suit when worn with the jacket.

Dory was putting her own clothes back on when the saleswoman brought another dress to the dressing room. "This was on the sale rack. It's probably not exactly what you want for the office, but it's so feminine I thought maybe..."

The dress was a drop-waist style in a muted white floral print on a pale salmon background. The wide, white collar was edged with lace. Dory hesitated, then said, "Why not? I'll try it."

She was standing in front of the mirror debating a few moments later when the saleslady returned. "It's pretty on you."

"It's so different from what I usually wear," Dory said.

"Why don't you let your husband take a look at it?"

"Oh, he's...he's really not interested in clothes," Dory said, deciding not to correct the natural but erroneous assumption.

"He's certainly been attentive today," the saleslady said. "So complimentary."

"He's trying to make me feel good," Dory said, smiling. "I felt..."

"Like a bloated toad?" the saleswoman said with a chuckle. "It's perfectly normal. You know, you'd be able to wear that dress another couple of months, at least. And then afterward...it's always nice to have something a little frilly and feminine to wear after the baby gets here. Why don't you show it to him, ask what he thinks."

Scott liked it immediately, and Dory took the role of devil's advocate. "It's really not for the office."

Scott kissed her on the cheek. "Get it. You can wear it to brunch tomorrow."

"I knew he'd like it," the saleswoman said, as she waited outside the dressing-room stall for Dory to pass her the dress so she could put it on one of the special hangers that fit in the dress bags the store used. "It's so refreshing to see young people who care about each other. The way he looks at you—" She sighed dramatically. "Takes me back thirty years. My husband used to say I glowed when I was pregnant."

Dory handed her the dress. "I'll go ring this up with the others, and we'll have everything ready to go by the time you're dressed."

"Wait!" Dory said. "My credit card—"

"But your husband—"

"He doesn't like carrying a wallet full of cards, and since I was going to have my purse today, I brought mine instead."

The saleslady took the card that Dory poked through the partially opened door, and looked down at it. "I'll have it all written up and waiting for your signature."

Still in her underwear, Dory sat down on the corner stool in the stall and buried her face in her hands. *It was none of her business*, she thought fiercely, but she still felt dishonest, hypocritical over the misconception she hadn't straightened out and the white lie she'd told.

Scott's radar picked up on her drooping morale immediately. With the hangers of her new clothes looped round his fingers and the heavy plastic clothes bag riding on his back, he said, "You don't look like a woman who's just bought out the store."

"I'm tired," she said, realizing how lame the excuse sounded, and how ingrained that catch-all phrase was becoming in her vocabulary.

"We've only got one more stop."

She gave him a quizzical look. "So what are we shopping for?"

"You'll see," he said, cupping her elbow to guide her as they walked through the department store.

"I think the men's department is back—"

"We're not going to the men's department."

"Then what—"

He stopped suddenly and gave her a bedroom smile. "Here we are."

Dory's jaw fell slack. They were on the edge of the lingerie and sleepwear department. "Scott?"

"Come on," he said, bobbing his head. "We've still got shopping to do."

She followed as he stepped from the aisle onto the thick carpet and moved from one display mannequin to another, stopping from time to time to lift a skirt of sheer chiffon or sleek satin into his fingers and examine it critically. "What are you doing?" Dory whispered.

"I'm going to buy you something sexy," he answered in a jovial whisper that mocked hers.

"I don't need—Do you know how much I've spent today?"

"As much as you're going to spend," he said. "Now I want to buy you something. A present."

"Why?"

The question amused him, and he chuckled. "Because you're beautiful." He leaned forward and spoke into her ear, "And because I love seeing you in sexy things."

A salesclerk approached and asked tactfully, "Are you folks finding what you need?"

Dory would have answered that they were just looking, but Scott spoke sooner. "We're looking for the sexiest nightie you've got."

"I see," the woman said.

She obviously saw too much for Dory's peace of mind. Dory put her hand on Scott's arm and gave it a significant pinch.

Undaunted, Scott said, "Something you can see through. And something loose. You know...flowing."

"Diaphanous?" the woman suggested.

Scott turned to Dory. "Isn't that the word the senator used?"

"Did you say the senator?" the clerk asked.

"You weren't supposed to hear that!" Scott said.

"Scott!" Dory said under her breath, straining the censure through her teeth. She was very close to laughing . . . or crying.

Ignoring her, Scott devoted full attention to the clerk and said, "You were going to show us something diaphanous?"

"Of course," she said. "Did you want something short—in a baby doll, or midlength or something to the floor."

"To the floor, I think," Scott said.

Dory clamped her teeth together and followed Scott and the salesclerk to a circular rack in the center of the department.

"Size?"

Scott gave Dory a sultry, evaluative top-of-head to tip-of-toes going-over and grinned at her affably, as her face turned crimson. "Medium."

The clerk pulled out a blue gown in a Grecian design with a bodice that hung in draped criss-crosses of fabric. It had a tie belt of satin ribbon.

Scott shook his head at the fitted waist. "How about something a little more—" he used his free hand to make a flamboyant gesture "—loose. You know, something that moves. Something . . . diaphanous."

"This is elegant," the clerk said, pulling out an empire-waist gown with a circular skirt of pleated white chiffon that spread from a yoke of silver-colored satin tulip-motif appliqués. "This is a popular choice for bridal trousseaus."

Scott pinched a pleat of the skirt and lifted it. The chiffon seemed to drop into an endless flow of fabric, full, yet delicate. "This is definitely diaphanous," he said. He aimed a mischievous wink at Dory. "The senator will be pleased. We'll take it."

"I'll put it in a box for you," the clerk said, gathering it into her arms to carry it to the sales counter.

Dory anchored Scott by looping her arm through his and tugging. "That gown is almost two hundred dollars!" she grated through clenched teeth.

"I guess it's a good thing I stopped at the automatic teller earlier, huh?"

She sniffed exasperatedly. "Scott!"

"I'm going to enjoy seeing you wear it." He leaned down to kiss the tip of her nose. "Even when you get to the point where you look like you swallowed a watermelon!"

"I THINK you blew the senator cover when you kissed me," Dory said on the way to the car.

"Naw," he said, with a shake of his head. "Did you see her expression when I told her I was paying cash? No one pays cash unless they're hiding something. It's probably driving her crazy. She's probably on the phone right now describing you, trying to figure out what senator's keeping you."

"You're cruel," Dory said. "Absolutely merciless. And..."

They reached the car. Scott still had the dresses hooked over the fingers of one hand and was holding the coat box with the gown in it under his opposite arm. "Dig my keys out of my pocket, would you?"

"Nice try," Dory said, pulling the box out from under his arm. "Get your own keys, Casanova."

Scott unlocked the car door, spread the dresses on the back seat and wedged the box on the floor, then stuck his face inches from Dory's. "And?"

"And what?"

"You were listing all my bad traits," he said. "We got through cruel and merciless before you were interrupted. You were about to add—"

"Wonderful," she said, wrapping her arms around his neck. "A little bit *strange* sometimes, but wonderful."

"WE SHOULD BE HAVING champagne and caviar," Dory said.

"Neither of us likes caviar, I don't care for champagne, and you're on the wagon for the duration," Scott replied.

"Mere technicalities," Dory said, reaching for her chocolate shake. "When a woman's having a picnic in the middle of the bed in the middle of the night wearing a two-hundred-dollar *diaphanous* nightgown, she should be eating caviar and chopped boiled eggs."

"You're doing quite well on the French fries and a Big Mac," Scott said.

Dory smiled at him from behind the straw in her waxed cup. "This *was* a wonderful idea. You're a genius for thinking of it."

He looked at her, sitting there on the bed with the white chiffon swirling round her like a cloud. The satin yoke covered her breasts, but small spaces left between the flowers gave him enticing peeps at the smooth skin beneath. "I'm glad you woke up," he said.

"For a man who could break into a house and steal into bed without waking the mistress of the house, you were trumping around the bedroom like an elephant."

He leaned forward to kiss her briefly. "Maybe I wanted to wake you up because I wanted company, even though I didn't realize that was what I was doing."

"You mean subconsciously?"

"That's it," he said. "Subconsciously."

"You've got to watch that old subconscious," Dory warned gravely. "Sometimes it plays some real tricks."

"Tonight, I'm grateful."

She smiled. "So am I."

When she'd first put on the gown and looked in the mirror, Dory had remembered the salesclerk saying that it was a popular choice for bridal trousseaus and wondered how it felt to be a bride. Then, when she'd gone into the living room wearing the sheer garment, slightly self-conscious about the new roundness of her body, which would be so obviously silhouetted by the sheer chiffon, she'd known.

Scott had looked at her with awe in his eyes. Awe and fascination and desire, and Dory had thought, *This must be the way it used to be when brides were virgins and grooms were nervous.*

Their lovemaking had been sweeter and slower than she'd ever remembered it. She'd fallen asleep in Scott's arms and woke up to discover him dressing to go to McDonald's. He was hungry. Suddenly, she'd been hungry too, and asked him to bring her a Big Mac, fries and a shake. Then, while he was gone, she'd spread her red-and-white checked tablecloth over the bed for their impromptu picnic.

"We're never going to get back to sleep again after all this food," Dory said as Scott stuffed the tablecloth into the dirty clothes hamper in the final phase of cleanup. But five minutes after he'd climbed back into bed they were both sleeping soundly, cuddled together under the covers like puppies who'd just drunk their fill of warm mother's milk.

Several hours later a deep voice stirred her. She sighed something unintelligible and nudged closer to Scott.

"Dory." Scott's voice again, more insistent. She grudgingly opened one eye and made a sound that might have been loosely interpreted as, "Huh?"

"Dory, is the baby moving?"

Dory was still a moment and felt the strong quickening in her womb. "Yes," she murmured. "He kicks like that all the time, especially in the morning."

Scott released a chuckle of delighted amazement. "I felt him. It woke me up." He spread his hand over her abdomen. "I can't believe he's so strong."

"He's saying thank-you for the hamburger."

"How big is it? Do you know?"

"About nine inches long."

"We could see it. Without a microscope or anything, I mean."

Dory grinned at his naïveté, his sudden endearing curiosity. "Yes. It's a tiny human being, a miniature of what it'll look like when it's born. We could even tell whether it's a boy or a girl."

"When will we know for sure?"

This time, Dory laughed. "When it's born. There are tests they could take, but since I'm not considered at risk, there's no need to run any of them. So unless the baby is turned just right when they do an ultrasound—"

"That sounds like something out of science fiction."

"It's similar to an X ray, but they use sound waves to get an image. There's no radiation."

"You'll tell me, won't you? If they find out?"

"If you want to know."

"I want to know everything, Dory."

There was a short silence. Dory swallowed. "Scott...in our class we discussed labor. I need to know what you want me to do. Do you want me to call you when I go into labor, or wait...."

"When you go into labor, of course. I want to—" He stopped, not knowing how to finish the sentence, not sure what he wanted to do. "How long does it take?"

"It varies," Dory said. "Usually it takes at least eight hours for the first time. But it could be quicker, or longer."

"I'll come as soon as you call me."

Uncomfortable with the conversation, she looked away from him, staring at his chest instead of his face. The loss of intimacy disturbed him. Her forefinger idly traced circles and curlicues on his chest, but it was no compensation.

"I'm learning breathing to make it easier, but I'm no hero," she said. "I'll probably be a first-class chicken and have them give me something right away, so I probably won't even know whether you're there until you tell me later."

He heard the lie in her voice, and it sundered his heart. She wanted him there and knew he couldn't assure her he would be. She was trying to protect him, shield him from guilt. He felt the frustration of not being able to reassure her, the shame that she felt the need to protect him. For the first time since he was a child, he felt like crying.

After a long silence, he said, "I've got an appointment with an attorney tomorrow," he said. That much he could give her. "I would have gone sooner, but he's been on vacation."

"I'll be expecting the contract, then."

Another long silence stretched between them before she said, "My internal clock's all confused. What time is it?"

Scott had no idea what time it was, either. Maybe, he thought, hours were meaningless. Maybe one day you woke up and it was just time.

14

SCOTT HADN'T WANTED to leave. It was more than the usual reluctance to relinquish their time together, more than the regret that they spent so little time in each other's lives. Usually by the time he was well onto the interstate he was already thinking ahead—of his work load at the office, of assignments he would give his classes. Usually his life away from her came rushing back in to fill the empty space his leaving her had created. But this time was different. This time the regret bit deeper into his heart, and an avalanche of tax returns and ungraded papers promised poor compensation for losing Dory's warm body next to his in bed and her smile flashing sunshine at him at unexpected moments.

He stopped at the supermarket for cold cuts to put together a meal that would be abysmally solitary. The couple in front of him at the checkout had a child who sat in the seat in the shopping cart gnawing on the plastic wrapping on a block of cheese. Scott perused the child's young face alternately with those of his parents, searching for common denominators in their features, answers to genetic riddles. He had felt his own child move; now he wondered what that child would look like.

He did not sleep well, a phenomenon he chalked up to the weird schedule he'd kept over the weekend, so he was not in the best of moods when he entered the attorney's office on Monday afternoon with fatigue and embarrassment sitting on his shoulders.

The attorney, Sydney Tabor, introduced himself and asked Scott to summarize why he'd come. Despite the lawyer's insistence on being called Syd and moving to a chummy, first-name basis, Scott was uncomfortable. "The woman I've been . . . seeing . . . for three years is pregnant."

There was an awkward pause. Scott shifted in his chair.

Scott's discomfort aside, it was business as usual for Syd. He sounded bored as he asked, "How much does she want?"

"I beg your pardon?" Scott said.

"Has she given you a specific dollar amount?"

The whole thing seemed uglier than ever to Scott, and more embarrassing than he'd dreaded. He tried to explain. "She hasn't asked for money. She's an attorney, so she thought—" He cleared his throat, and unconsciously pulled at his tie. "She suggested that I might want to get something about paternal rights in writing. As a protection."

"Um-hm," Syd said, as noncommittally as the doctors in an old television sitcom.

"She thought that if something happened to her, I would want some legal recourse in taking care of the child."

"The child will live with the mother?"

"Yes."

"Then you agree that the mother will be the primary custodial parent?" Syd said, writing furiously on a pad of yellow paper.

"Yes. But I'll be visiting regularly."

"We'll get to visitation rights later," Syd said. "You say that you want legal protection of your rights as the child's father?"

Scott nodded.

"Then I suggest that we make joint parental responsibility part of your agreement with the mother. This would give you legal authority to, say, have the child admitted to a hospital, or see the child's school records."

"Couldn't I do that as the child's father anyway?"

"Without joint parental responsibility, you could be subject to the goodwill of the mother, and, in the event of her incapacitation or death, the whim of the court."

Syd gave Scott a piercing look. "Joint parental responsibility will protect your rights in case of substantial changes in your relationship with the mother. For instance, if either of you should marry someone else—"

"There's no chance of that. Dory and I would never—"

"Or if either of you should relocate, you'd still want to maintain contact with the child."

"Relocate?"

"The mother could move anywhere in the world and take the child with her, unless you have some sort of safeguard," Syd said. He scratched at the legal pad again furiously. "I think we should put in some provision about prior notification if the mother should decide to move out of state."

"Dory grew up in Tallahassee. Her family's there. She would never leave. Otherwise, she might have moved to Gainesville years ago."

Syd ignored his protests. "Do you want to set up a schedule of child support payments?" Before Scott could answer, he continued, "It would be a good idea for a number of reasons. A willingness to assume financial responsibility for the child would create a sympathetic hearing for any future requests for structured visitation rights, or similar requests."

Scott was numb. *Child support? Visitation rights?* It was beginning to sound like a divorce settlement.

"Did you have any specific amount in mind?" Syd asked.

Scott shrugged to indicate he hadn't. "What's standard?"

"There are variables, of course. Your overall financial situation and the mother's. I suggest that you decide what you feel to be the maximum equitable figure, and we'll cut it in half for the original contract. That way we'll have room for negotiation. We'll be able to give a little and still come out ahead."

"I want to be fair," Scott said. "Dory won't ask—"

The attorney grinned wryly. Obviously he thought he was dealing with a fool.

Scott held the balls of the chair arms in a death grip as he squelched the urge to punch the supercilious expression off the worm's face. "Look, Dory's concern was that if something happened to her, I would want some legal documentation so that I could have a voice in what happened to the child."

Syd seemed not to notice Scott glowering at him and continued, unruffled, "It's within your rights to request the appropriate blood tests following the birth of the child."

"Blood tests?" Scott asked.

"To medically establish paternity. Actually they're more apt to rule out fatherhood than establish it, but—"

"I don't need any test results to tell me this is my baby," Scott said.

Syd looked skeptical. "You trust this woman then?"

Scott's ears burned with the force of his fury. The idea of Dory and another man—Dory lying to him—was ludicrous. Obviously Syd was jaded. He'd probably never met a decent woman in his life.

"Dory wouldn't . . . There's no question of infidelity," Scott said.

Syd held up his hands in a halting gesture. "That's between you and her. You know this woman. If you're willing to accept responsibility without tests, then we won't make the request." He gave Scott a stern look. "You should, though, insist that you be listed as the father on the birth certificate. Do you want to make this request in writing, or present it to the mother verbally?"

"I'll talk to her," Scott said.

"I would advise you to have her agree to do this in writing. A notarized letter would be sufficient."

Scott nodded. "Is there anything else?" he asked petulantly.

"Not today," Syd said. "Except to come up with an amount of support. I'll get this into contract form and we'll send it to the mother for approval and negotiate any points of disagreement."

A frown hardened Scott's lips. There it was again. Legal jargon.

"I would suggest that, after all the details are finalized, we present the agreement to the court for ratification in the county where she lives. Court ratification would add weight to any of the terms, in the event of future disputes."

Still frowning, Scott nodded grave agreement.

SCOTT ROWLAND, JUNIOR, was not a happy man when he stamped into his office Tuesday morning after a second sleepless night. He answered Mike's benign "Good morning" with a skeptical "Who says so?"

Mike followed him to the coffee maker, where Scott filled his mug. "Milk sour in your refrigerator this morning?"

Scott gave him a seething scowl. "Please, Mike. I don't need any smart remarks."

"Sorry," Mike said. He trailed Scott to his office, where Scott dropped into the chair behind his desk and took a deep draft of coffee. Mike took the client's seat facing the desk. "You got problems?"

Scott put down his cup and combed his right hand through his hair in a gesture of despair. Heaving a sigh, he said, "I'm up to my ass in alligators."

"Trouble at the school?" Mike asked. The regents had been dangling tenure in front of Scott's nose for two years in a peculiar game of campus politics that Scott was disinclined to play.

Scott propped his elbow on the desk and braced his forehead with his fingertips. "School's fine."

"So what alligators you got snapping at you?"

"A whole swampful," Scott said. "Starting with a mealy-mouthed shyster."

"Benton?" Mike asked curiously, referring to the attorney the firm retained.

"No. Sydney Tabor. Syd." He sniffed disdainfully. "I tell you, Mike, you can't trust professors. They're illiterates when it comes to real life."

"I've always found the whole bunch of them to be an unstable lot," Mike said dourly.

"I made a special trip over to the law school to ask Tom Morden—you remember him, he teaches theory of law—to recommend someone competent, and he sends me to an ambulance chaser named Syd. Syd! Heaven help the American justice system if Syd Tabor is the best they've got."

"You got legal problems?" Mike asked.

Scott leveled his eyes on his best friend's face. He had to tell someone, sometime. It might as well be his best friend, now. "Dory's pregnant."

"Holy..." Mike said. "When...how long have you known?"

"Since before Thanksgiving."

Mike whistled and said, "No wonder you've been squirming around trying to find some reason not to marry her."

"Dory and I don't want to get married."

"Have you asked Dory about that lately?"

"I offered to marry her the night she told me."

"I'll just bet you bowled her over with candlelight and roses."

Mike's sarcasm hurt. His defection was a devastating blow. It seemed to Scott that the world was ganging up against him in some sinister conspiracy designed to make him feel like a heel. "If you've got something to say why don't you just spit it out?" he challenged.

"All right, I will. You're about as close to a brother as I'll ever have, so I'll talk to you the way I'd talk to a brother. You may be a genius when it comes to mathematics, but you're an idiot when it comes to Dory."

"You know how it is between Dory and me!"

"Don't you think a baby changes things a little?"

"Of course it does!" Scott said. That was the hell of it—that it changed something that was perfect! "That's why I was at Sydney Shyster's setting up child support and getting 'joint parental responsibility.'"

"But you're not going to marry her."

"If I wanted someone to nag me, I'd marry Dory, not listen to you!"

"Well, someone needs to nag you. Dory never would. She loves you too much, but you're too blind to see that."

"I don't think this is any of your business."

"You're my best friend. And Dory—well, let's say I think Dory's a pretty special lady, and it galls me to see you treating her like swamp scum."

"Would you like to get out of my office before our friendship—not to mention our partnership—gets blown to hell and back?"

"No," Mike said. "I'm not going to get out until I say my piece. I've been holding it too long."

"By all means, then, say your piece!" Scott said, crossing his arms over his chest and giving Mike a belligerent glare.

"You should have married her a long time ago," Mike said. "If I was her brother, instead of your best friend, I'd probably have beat the pulp out of you by now, trying to knock some sense into you where she's concerned."

"You sound like a Victorian guardian."

"Decency doesn't go out of style," Mike said. "What the hell are you waiting on?"

"You know how I feel about marriage."

Mike shook his head slowly. "You're something, you know that? For a genius, you're a flaming idiot. How long are you going to go on penalizing Dory for the mess your parents made of their lives?"

"You're out of line, Mike. And you're wrong."

"Am I? Tell me what marriage you've ever seen up close that wasn't a catastrophe."

"There's yours."

"Yes. There's mine. And you can't stand the fact that I'm happy being married."

Scott fixed a glare on Mike's face. "You're my best friend. I'm *delighted* you and Susan—"

"You resent the hell out of the fact that Susan and I are happy, because we shoot your there's-no-such-thing-as-a-happy-marriage theory right out of the water," Mike accused. "We're making you nervous."

"Nervous?"

"Yeah. Because if it works for us, it might work for you and Dory. And that's scaring the hell out of you."

An awkward silence filled the room before Mike went on. "Why are you fighting it so hard? Why can't you just admit that you want to marry her?"

"Because—" Scott sputtered, then desperately started over. "I don't . . ."

"Don't love her?" Mike challenged.

"You know I love Dory!"

"Then you don't like being with her?"

"I love being with Dory. I just don't want it to be a command performance every night at six."

"What is it, Scott? You got more important things to do?"

"I just . . ."

"What's more important than Dory, Scott? Partying? Watching football on big screens in bars? You got some coeds you're holing up with somewhere?"

"What is this? An inquisition? You know I don't play around on Dory. I've never been unfaithful to her."

"You love her. You aren't interested in other women. What's your big objection to getting married like normal people?"

"I'm scared of ruining it!" Scott said. "Now it's . . . we're together because we choose to be."

Mike shook his head slowly. "You're the stubbornest, most selfish jerk I've ever had for a best friend. And the blindest."

A muscle twitched in Scott's jaw as he chomped down on anger. Through gritted teeth he said, "Thanks, *pal*."

Mike's tone mellowed, and the softness with which he spoke gave his words a special force. "I just hate seeing you blow it, *pal*. You're crazy in love with her, and you're going to lose her through sheer cussedness."

The scowl on Scott's face gradually faded into a frown.

Mike continued. "Maybe you don't think marriage is as important as freedom. Maybe that little piece of paper called a marriage certificate doesn't mean anything to you. Maybe it's never meant anything to Dory up to now. But let me tell you something, friend, eventually the lack of it is going to mean everything to Dory and that baby she's carrying. You'd better think about that, *pal*."

The silence was overwhelming, oppressive. "You are thinking about it, aren't you?" Mike persisted. "You've been thinking about it, and it's tearing you apart, because your pride's getting in the way."

"Yeah," Scott said bitterly, remembering the argument he'd had with Dory over his macho ego. "My damned, stupid pride."

"Well, think about this—when that baby's just a little bitty thing, nothing's going to matter to it besides where the next bottle comes from. But that baby's going to grow into a child, and that child is going to look at Dory and say, 'Mommy, why doesn't Daddy live with us like the other daddies?' And Dory's going to start thinking about how much a kid deserves a daddy, and she might just start shopping for one for her child."

"What the hell's that supposed to mean? You been conferring with Sydney Shyster?"

"It's human nature, Scott. Dory's smart enough to raise a dozen babies by herself, but that doesn't mean she'd want to. And why should she? She's bright and attractive and likable—why should she settle for doing it alone? No matter what you hear about the man shortage, there are plenty of men who'd leap at the chance to settle down with a woman with Dory's qualities."

A sickness settled over Scott. He was a small boy again, asking his mother if his daddy was dead, wondering why his father had gone away. The pain wrenched his guts and choked his throat closed. And on the heels of that venerable pain came the debilitating fear of a man who loved a woman and faced losing her.

Mike said compassionately, "It's sad, Scott—you sitting there mentally beating up on yourself because you love her and you want to spend your life with her. The irony is that you're so hung up with freedom of choice that you're too blind to realize that you've been married to Dory in your heart for years."

Surprise passed over Scott's face, and Mike responded to it with a chortle of laughter. "You didn't even realize it, did you? In some ways—a lot of important ways—you're as married to her as I am to Susan. You're crazy about her. You're faithful to her. The only thing you don't do is go home to her every night, and what would be so awful about that?" He turned to leave, but stopped in the doorway and looked back at Scott. "Marry her, Scott. It's not so bad being bitched at because you want a fish sandwich in the middle of the night."

Scott stared down at his desk and said sheepishly, "Dory doesn't care if I go to McDonald's in the middle of the night as long as I bring her back a Big Mac and fries." *She spreads a tablecloth for a picnic.*

Mike laughed aloud. "You tried it. You actually tried it. That's rich, Scott. You tried to hang her with my wife's peccadilloes, and it didn't work."

"I wasn't trying to do anything. I just woke up hungry, and . . ."

"You were trying to hang her with the institution of marriage. You tried to catch her at being imperfect, and she wouldn't cooperate." Mike's mirth had faded. "Marry her, Scott. You'll find her little imperfections and love her in spite of them. Go home every night and kiss her hello and bounce that baby on your knee and let it know it's got a daddy who loves it."

Scott stared at the empty doorway after Mike left and felt very alone. He went through the motions of trying to work, automatically switching on the computer. The command prompts flashed onto the screen of the monitor but went unread, because Scott was seeing only Dory's face. Dory, so fiercely independent that she asked for nothing except that he not ignore their child. Dory, pregnant, but not clinging or demanding. Dory, giving, caring, loving. Dory, the tough and competent attorney who baked him blueberry muffins with fresh blueberries. Dory, who'd courageously started making room for their child in her life without grudge or resentment. Dory, holding a child in her arms, cradling its head on her shoulder.

Squinting, Scott strained to see the child's face, but his mind failed to provide the image, denying him because he didn't deserve to see the child he'd been denying. How could he have been so blind? He'd thought Dory was excluding him, shutting him out, but she'd only been respecting his wishes, shielding him from responsibility he'd been too gutless to assume.

Scott no longer wanted to be shielded from responsibility. He wanted, in every cell of his body and mind, to be an integral part of Dory's life, of their child's. He'd spent much of his life excluded, the eternal outsider in two households, the child who didn't belong to his father and his father's wife or to his mother and her new husband. His stepsiblings—his father's two sons and his mother's daughter—had belonged, but Scott had been the barely tolerated stepchild in both households.

Now his choices came to him as clearly as if they were displayed in Queen's English on the computer monitor. He could remain the outsider, or he could go to

Dory and be a part of the family. His family. Their family, his and Dory's and the baby's.

In his mind, he saw Dory as she had been Saturday, sitting on the bed in her flowing white gown, hair mussed, eating French fries in the middle of the night. As she had been on New Year's Day, lying next to him on the floor in front of the fireplace, her eyes glistening with awed excitement when she felt their baby move. He understood that excitement now, the overflowing of love for a tiny, innocent life he'd help to create. Perhaps he hadn't been able to feel that tiny evidence of life on New Year's Day because he hadn't been ready to accept it. Now he was.

He clicked off the computer and stood up, pushing the chair free of the desk with the backs of his knees in an abrupt motion. He went to Mike's office, stopped in the doorway until he caught Mike's eye. "I've got to go to the school early to take care of some loose ends, and I'll be out tomorrow, maybe even Thursday."

Mike nodded understanding. Not just comprehension, Scott thought, but genuine understanding. What he'd been cheated out of as a child, he'd been compensated for in adulthood. A friend like Mike—a woman like Dory. What had he given them of himself to deserve the part of themselves they shared so freely with him?

Scott leveled his eyes on his friend's face. "You still game to open that branch office in Tallahassee we've always joked about?"

"Know anyone reliable who's interested in moving to Tallahassee to run it?" Mike replied.

"It's our company," Scott answered. "It should be one of us."

Mike grinned at him knowingly. "You volunteering?"

"Yeah," Scott said, grinning back, no longer threatened or violated by what his friend could see in him. "I'm volunteering."

Mike's grin grew into laughter. "Tell Dory hello for me."

15

DORY WAS NOT AT THE HOUSE when Scott arrived. Battling a keen sense of letdown, Scott carried his hanging bag of clothes and shaving kit to the bedroom. If she wasn't home by the time he freshened up, he'd call her office to see if she was working late. The idea brought a frown to his lips. She needed to be getting plenty of rest, not putting in overtime.

He telephoned the office, although he no longer expected her to be there. The towel on the bar nearest the shower had been noticeably damp, and one of the new dresses she'd bought the preceding weekend had been sprawled across the bed as though she'd changed clothes quickly and not bothered to hang it up or put it in the hamper. If he'd been a little earlier, he probably would have caught her. Maybe he shouldn't have taken the little detour he'd taken, but when he'd been able to leave his teaching assistant in charge of his class, he'd thought his timing would be perfect.

He tried the office, just in case. A machine answered the ring, detailing the hours the office was open and inviting the caller to leave a message at the sound of the beep. He spoke into the machine in case Dory had gone back there and was monitoring calls. When she didn't grab the phone, he sat back to wait for her.

An hour crawled by, an hour in which Scott imagined a hundred places Dory might be and reflected on the fact that, despite having known her so long and so intimately, he actually knew little about her daily routines when they were apart. Did she shop during the week? Take in an occasional movie? Lectures at the library? Go to dinner with clients? She belonged to a professional support group—did it meet evenings, or had she said they had breakfast meetings?

She could be late getting home. The prospect dismayed him. His decision had been so long in the making and was so monumental in importance that he was anxious to confront her, share his realizations, his dreams and his innermost feelings. Newly aware of how incomplete he was without her, he longed for the completion she brought to him. He wanted to ask if she felt the same way, the emptiness when he was gone, the fullness when they were together. They'd never lacked for conversation, but they had more to talk about now than ever before.

They needed to talk about forever.

After another quarter hour, it occurred to him that she might be with Sergei. She had mentioned once that he'd come to dinner; maybe she'd gone to his place.

He found Sergei's number in her address book. A rather sexy voice informed him that he had reached Dr. Sergei Karol's answering service, and that Dr. Karol was not in. Did he care to leave a message?

"Can you reach him right away?" Scott asked, thinking it would be futile to leave a message if Sergei didn't get it until the following morning.

"Is this a medical emergency?"

"No. No emergency. It's a personal call, but it is important. If you talk to him tonight, would you please tell him Scott called from his sister's house?"

"I'll see what I can do," the woman replied.

Sergei returned the call immediately. "Scott!" he said frantically. "Is Dory okay? Is it the baby?"

"They're both fine, as far as I know. I just came into town to surprise Dory, and she's not home. I thought maybe she was with you, or that you might know where she is."

"You scared the hell out of me!" Sergei snapped.

"I told your service it wasn't an emergency," Scott said, and added a meek, "Sorry."

"Dory's not with me," Sergei said.

"Do you know where she might be?"

"No, I...she didn't mention anything to me...wait! I think her childbirth preparatory classes are on Tuesday and Thursday."

"Where are they?"

"At the hospital."

"Think she'd mind if I dropped in?"

Sergei's voice took on an edge of challenge. "What are you doing here in the middle of the week, Scott?"

"I hope—with the proper cooperation from your sister—that I'm about to gain a surgeon for a brother-in-law."

"Then go for it!"

"Sergei?"

"What?"

"Thanks for not beating the hell out of me for being such a jerk."

"I had that penciled in on my calendar for the end of next month if you hadn't come around by then."

"Think she'll say yes?"

"I think she'll say it so loud I'll hear it on the other side of town."

Spirits buoyed, Scott whistled as he drove to the hospital and very nearly kissed the woman at the central desk who gave him directions to the room where the classes were being held.

He found the room easily. The door opened with a sucking sound, and he walked in to find it dark except for a low light turned toward the back wall. A dozen couples were sprawled on the floor, lying on exercise mats with their heads on pillows, listening to a recording of ocean waves.

A woman, obviously the instructor, since she was the only person not reclining, dashed to stop him before he disrupted the class. She took him to the most isolated corner of the room. "We have a class going on here," she whispered.

"I'm looking for Dory Karol," he whispered back.

"Unless it's an emergency, you'll have to—"

"It's an emergency," he whispered intensely. With his eyes adjusted to the light, he had spied Dory on one of the mats. He headed toward her, trying to be light on his feet despite the purpose in his stride.

Dory's eyes were closed, but the woman on the mat next to hers—the nurse who was her partner, he decided—saw him approaching and pushed up on one elbow, pressing the forefinger of her free hand to her lips to warn him not to disturb Dory. Scott knelt next to the mat and whispered into the woman's ear. "It's okay—I'm the father. I'll take it from here."

The woman's forehead crinkled in concentration as she debated what to do.

"Trust me," Scott whispered and gave her a charming smile before adding, "I love her."

Shaking her head, the woman moved silently to her feet and tiptoed across the room, leaving the mat for him.

DORY WAS AT THE OCEAN. The sun was warm on her face, the sea breeze refreshing as it teased through her hair. She was breathing deeply of that brine-cleansed air. Her body was relaxed, her arms and legs heavy on the mat, yet she felt herself floating as the tension weighting her muscles eased with each deep breath. Graduate of a self-hypnosis seminar and veteran hypnosis-tape listener, she was capable of relaxing quickly and thoroughly through visualization and concentration.

From somewhere, though, there came conflicting sensual messages. She was not smelling brine air, but Scott's after-shave. The even rhythm of Scott's breathing worked its way into the waves. Instead of the breeze in her hair, it was Scott's fingers gently stroking.

A smile curved her lips. It had happened before, this invasion of her visualizations. She simply changed the images to suit the fantasy, imagined that Scott had joined her at the beach, that he was looking at her with loving eyes. One of her slow, deep exhalations became a sensual sigh.

His lips touched hers, light as the passage of silk across satin. And then he was kissing her in earnest, savoring the shape of her lips with his tongue, pressing past them, testing the warm, marble smoothness of her teeth. Her eyes flew open. *This* had never happened before.

Wonderfully, miraculously, he was there, not a mere mental image but a man, warm, solid and strong. She gasped. Then, overcoming the shock, she wrapped her arms around his neck and cradled his face in her hands, hoping to resume the kiss. Her mind was still lethargic with relaxation, differentiating fantasy and reality with fuzzy distinction, but her body was strangely receptive to sensual stimuli. She parted her teeth in invitation, but Scott drew away from her until his face hovered inches above hers, frustratingly inaccessible.

"Will you marry me?"

The question had an instant sobering effect on her. Scott had had the awareness of surroundings and situation to whisper, so as not to disturb anyone around them, but Dory, coming out of deep relaxation, did not, and spoke with an excited fullness of voice. "Oh, Scott, are you sure? Is it what you want?"

Scott laughed aloud, no longer mindful of the class that now had been irretrievably disrupted. "Yes," he said and repeated the reply for good measure, louder, more distinctly.

Dory squealed with enough glee to rouse any cadavers in the hospital morgue, lurched into a sitting position, threw her arms around his neck and came close to shouting, "I love you."

The room lights came on while they were kissing, but neither noticed. They noticed nothing but each other, in fact, until the sound of applause penetrated the fog of exultation. They broke the kiss and, with their arms still around each other, looked around the room sheepishly at their appreciative audience.

"We're going to get married," Scott announced.

A pandemonium of congratulations and well-wishing followed. The teacher dismissed class early because there was no hope of anyone relaxing for a long, long time, and suggested they meet at a nearby pub to toast the bride and groom properly—with juice for the prospective mothers, of course.

Arms across each other's backs, Dory and Scott walked toward his car. "Are you sure?" Dory said. "What made you—"

Scott stopped in midstride and looked down at her face. "I suddenly realized that I'd rather have picnics with you in the middle of the night than get up and watch old movies on television."

Dory found that amusing, as he'd known she would, and he laughed with her. When their laughter faded, he touched her cheek with his fingertips and said, "I went to the attorney yesterday, and I realized how unnatural it is to have a contract stipulating that you have rights to a child. I want a family, not a legal arrangement."

"But a marriage license—we've always agreed we didn't need that, either."

"Can you look me in the eye and tell me you don't want a marriage license? And a home where we're all together?"

"No," she admitted in a whisper. "I want it. I've wanted it since the moment I accepted the fact that I was pregnant. Maybe even before."

He bent to brush her lips gently with his own. "I love you," he said. "I love our child. When you love someone, it makes more sense to have a piece of paper binding you to her, than one that takes care of the legal inconveniences of not being legally bound."

"Where will we live?"

"You're the lady with a house with a nursery in it. I guess I'll have to do the moving."

"But your firm—the university..."

"I'll open a branch here. And there's a college here. Maybe—"

"You? At Florida State?" Dory asked incredulously.

Scott grinned mischievously. "Amazing the depths a man will sink to to win the favor of his father-in-law, isn't it? The most important thing is that I love you, and I want to be with you. If you feel the same way, why don't you kiss me so we can go to the car and you can see your surprise."

"I'm not sure I can take another surprise," she said, before slipping her arms around his neck and kissing him solidly on the mouth. But, except for a few tears of joy, she coped very well with finding the wooden cradle from Micanopy in the back seat of Scott's car.

Later, amidst merrymaking at the pub, the class instructor predicted that Dory would be the first student in all her childbirth prep classes to be given a bridal shower by her fellow class members. Dory smiled beamingly and assured her it was all right, since she was probably also the first woman in the history of the world to get a semiantique baby cradle for an engagement present.

Everyone insisted on seeing the cradle, and Scott hauled it inside so they could examine and exclaim over it. Since they were all in the process of setting up nurseries, they were all immediately envious, even after Dory outlined all the inconveniences the shop owner had pointed out to her. The mother of the woman married to a cop assured her that designing a crib ensemble would be a piece of cake and offered to help Dory with it.

There was a toast to the cradle itself, and all the promise and sentiment contained in its wooden well. In the low light of the pub, Dory looked at the burnished wood and felt love and joy brim inside her, overflowing into every part of her. Her scalp, her fingertips, even her toes tingled with it. She and Scott were holding hands, and she threaded her fingers though his. A cradle was an unconventional engagement present, but their relationship had always been unconventional, so it was appropriate that their engagement should be. She saw the cradle as a symbol of their love: solid, sturdy, enduring.

The weather was crisp and cool, so she and Scott stopped for firewood on the way to the house, then lay in the darkness of the living room watching the dance of flames and shadows. While they were both aware of the tension rising in them, they did not hurry into lovemaking. They touched, kissed and talked, talked, kissed and touched, slipping without frenzy or hurry toward the physical expression of their love.

"I thought everything between us was perfect before," Scott said. "But it's different now. Better. How can you perfect perfection?"

"Maybe when something grows, there's more room for perfection," Dory said. She twisted slightly so that her abdomen pressed into his. "The baby's moving. Do you feel it?"

"Yes," Scott said, and on his cheeks the moisture of tears captured the glistening glow of the firelight.

Author's Note

JUDGE SCOTT ROWLAND was born at 4:55 a.m. on June 12, following a frenzied rush to the hospital by a composed mother and a frantic father-to-be. The actual labor lasted only two hours, and the birth was attended by the father at his loving best, Kate O'Banyan Sterling at her most efficient best and Dory's doctor at his most exasperated best.

Unfortunately while Dr. Sergei Karol arrived in plenty of time for the actual event, he fainted when the baby's head began crowning and had to be carried from the birthing room by two orderlies, an incident that would subject him to a great deal of ribbing at the hospital for years to come.

Scott and Dory selected the name Judge because they both liked movies by actor Judge Reinhold, but they conveniently neglected to mention their source of inspiration to the baby's maternal grandfather.

Little Judge was taken home and placed in the antique crib with George the Rabbit, a gift from his mother, and a plush alligator wearing a University of Florida jersey, a gift from his father. In the coming months Scott spent so much time trying to teach Judge how to say Gator that the baby began responding to the name himself. Thus, Judge Scott Rowland acquired a nickname that would stick with him for life.

If the nickname bothered Judge John Milford Karol, he gave no indication of it, for he proved to be an enthusiastic and doting granddaddy.

Mrs. Karol did not attempt to learn to knit, but she bought her grandson a recording of lullabies performed by the world's greatest symphonies and noted in the timbre of his cooing and cawing the promise of true musical potential.

Aunt Adelina announced early on that, while the baby was beautiful, her practice prohibited her offering to baby-sit, and on the first-month anniversary of Judge "Gator"'s birth she departed for New York to audition for the Metropolitan Opera, where she won a spot in the chorus. The following Christmas she sent her nephew a stuffed harlequin clown with a music box inside that played a passage from *I Pagliacci*.

On Christmas night Dory watched Scott rock Gator to sleep, moving the rocking chair in time to the tinkling music of the music box. When at last her son was asleep, she paused to appreciate the innocence of his cherubic face and the heartrending beauty of his dark eyelashes against his full cheeks. Then she went to her husband and bent to kiss his brow. "He's out like a light."

Scott put the baby to bed and joined his wife on the sofa in front of the fire for their private celebration.

◆HARLEQUIN
Temptation

COMING NEXT MONTH

#261 SOPHISTICATED LADY
Candace Schuler

As the model for an exclusive line of cosmetics, Samantha
Spencer wasn't so much attracted by fame and fortune as
she was by Alex Gavino's old-world charm. She knew he'd
hired her for her cool, sophisticated looks, unaware of the
fire under the ice. But once she took the wraps off, he'd
know what passion was all about....

#262 A STROKE OF GENIUS Gina Wilkins

Mallory Littlefield's gorgeous new boss, Elliott Frazer, was a
certified genius. But the poor man was completely
incompetent when it came to day-to-day life. Free-spirited
Mallory was soon teaching him everything she knew—from
driving a car to dancing. And it didn't take a high IQ to
guess where the lessons were leading.

#263 WHEN FORTUNE SMILES
Sally Bradford

When yuppie dentist Alex Carson invaded Gretchen
Bauer's apartment, lock, stock and jock equipment,
Gretchen became suspicious. She was in dire financial need,
so any roommate—male or female—was a godsend. But
Alex didn't have to count pennies. If he was planning to
share more than the rent, her home would soon be
transformed into a battleground... or a love nest....

#264 AN UNMARRIED MAN
Sarah Hawkes

Alec Lindfors thought posing as a married man would save
him from commitment-seeking women. But after meeting
Michelle, he didn't know if he *wanted* to be saved. Nor did
he know she was on to his little deception....

Have You Ever Wondered If You Could Write A Harlequin Novel?

Here's great news—Harlequin is offering a series of cassette tapes to help you do just that. Written by Harlequin editors, these tapes give practical advice on how to make your characters—and your story— come alive. There's a tape for each contemporary romance series Harlequin publishes.

Mail order only

All sales final

ANNOUNCING . . .

The Lost Moon Flower
by Bethany Campbell

Look for it this August
wherever Harlequins are sold

HR 3000-1